AUG -- 2001

DATE DUE

NOV 0 1 2001	
NOV 0 7 2001	
DEC 1 2 2001	
FEB 2 5 2002	
MAR 2 8 2002	
MAY 2 6 2002	
JUN 2 9 2002	
AUG 1 5 2002	
SEP 0 9 2002	

GAYLORD   PRINTED IN U.S.A.

THE
WONDERFUL
SKY BOAT

JANE LOUISE CURRY

THE WONDERFUL SKY BOAT

and **OTHER NATIVE AMERICAN TALES** *of the* **SOUTHEAST**

Illustrated

by

JAMES WATTS

MARGARET K. McELDERRY BOOKS

New York London Toronto Sydney Singapore

Margaret K. McElderry Books
An imprint of Simon & Schuster Children's Publishing Division
1230 Avenue of the Americas
New York, New York 10020

Book design by Michael Nelson
The text of this book is set in Guardi Roman.

Printed in the United States of America
2 4 6 8 10 9 7 5 3 1

Library of Congress Cataloging-in-Publication Data
The wonderful sky boat : and other Native American
tales of the Southeast / [compiled by] Jane Louise Curry;
illustrated by James Watts.
p. cm.
Includes bibliographical references.
ISBN 0-689-83595-7
1. Indians of North America—Southern States—Folklore.
2. Indian mythology—Southern States. 3. Tales—Southern States.
[1. Indians of North America—Southern States—Folklore.
2. Folklore—Southern States.] I. Curry, Jane Louise.
II. Watts, James, ill.
E78.S65 W65 2001
398.2'089'97—dc21   00-040207

FIRST **F** EDITION

For Isabella
—J. L. C.

For my godson, Jack, and Ryan and William
—J. W.

CONTENTS

Some of the Southeastern Peoples

ABOUT THE
SOUTHEASTERN TRIBES

The Southeast—South Carolina, Georgia, Florida, Alabama, Mississippi, Louisiana, western North Carolina and Virginia, southern Arkansas, the eastern fringe of Texas, and much of Tennessee—had in many ways the richest Native American culture in North America. Only the Southeastern tribes relied more on farming than on hunting and gathering. Farming gave many of them the prosperity to build large towns and meetinghouses. The region had a great variety and wealth of languages, ceremonies, dances, and arts—and tales.

More of the Southeastern peoples belonged to the Muskhogean language "family"—related tribes that spoke similar languages—than any other. Among their neighbors along the shores and borders of the Southeast, and among the latecomers to the region, were groups who spoke Siouan, Caddoan, and Iroquoian languages. Still others, like the Atakapa, Natchez, and Yuchi, had languages of their own. After the coming of the Europeans, the tales of many of these peoples vanished along with their tellers. For those who survived that invasion, the old way of life was lost. In time, most were uprooted and some took refuge with stronger neighbors, but they carried their stories with them, and their storytellers told the tales again and again down the long years. Perhaps, in the mountains of South Carolina, a Cherokee grandmother is telling one now. . . .

THE WONDERFUL SKY BOAT

THE CREATION OF THE WORLD

Yuchi

In the beginning, this world below the great dome of
the sky was nothing but water. The first bird and animal people, larger and more powerful than those we
know today, lived in the land above the dome of the
sky. Water-animal people lived in the waters below.
There was no earth at all, no world to stand on.

In time, the land above the sky dome grew
crowded. Some of the bird people began to com-
plain. "We need more room," the bird people said.
"We need a way to make a world for the animal
people down below, in the middle of the waters."

"But it takes earth to make a world," T-cho, the
Sun, said. "Where will we find earth? Everything
below is water."

Because no one knew the answer, the sky
people agreed to hold a council to decide what to
do. Sun led the meeting. "If there is any earth in the
world below," she said, "it must be beneath the waters.
But how are we to find it? You birds cannot fly
below the waters, and I must not touch them at all."

Crane spoke up. "Then we shall ask the animals
who live in the water to help."

"Perhaps Beaver will help," said Red-Bellied
Woodpecker. "He could live on land as well as water."

So the birds flew down to talk to the water people, and asked Beaver to dive down through the waters to find some earth to make a world. "I will do it!" Beaver cried, and he tried. He came up gasping. "I swam as deep as I could swim," he wheezed when he could speak. "If there is a bottom, I could not find it."

The bird people then asked Fish Otter to try to find the earth they needed. "I will do it!" Fish Otter agreed, and he slid down through the waters. He was out of sight much longer than Beaver, but he, too, came up gasping. "I swam as deep as I could," Fish Otter choked out when he could speak. "If there is a bottom, I could not find it."

After all the other water people had failed, the people from the land above the sky dome decided to ask the very last, Lock-chew, the crawfish. "Crawfish, will *you* dive down to find the bottom of the waters?"

Lock-chew was a careful fellow. "I can dive deep, so perhaps I can find earth for you," he said. "Perhaps not. You must watch for a sign. If I go so deep that I cannot come up again, you will see blood in the water. If I have found earth, I will stir it up with my tail and claws. You will see the water grow yellow with mud before you see me."

Crawfish was very small to dive so deep, but Sun and the bird people said, "Try." So he did. He swam down, down, down out of sight, and he was gone for a very long time. At last, the watchers saw yellowish water come swirling up. A while after that, Crawfish appeared, too, with a little dirt clutched in his claws.

Crawfish placed the crumb of soft earth on the top of the water. T-cho, the Sun, touched it. Then T-cho asked the bird people, "Who will spread this earth out across the water, and fan it dry?"

"Let Ah-yok, the Hawk, do it," some said. "The wind from his wings can spread it smooth and dry it, too."

"No," cried all the others. "The wings of Yah-tee, the Buzzard, are wider and stronger. He is the best one to do this work!"

It was agreed that Yah-tee should go, and that no one was to walk upon the new land until it was smooth and dry. So Yah-tee, the Buzzard, flew up high and began to soar over the bit of earth with wide swoops. He glided back and forth on his great wings, and at once the earth began to spread out in all directions. He flew and flew and flew, and it spread and spread and spread until it was the great island that is the earth today. "How beautiful and flat it is!" the bird and animal people cried. Yah-tee soared on, and the land began to dry in the soft wind from his passing. But then—*ai!* When the work was almost finished, Yah-tee's wings grew too tired to hold stretched out so wide and still for even a moment longer. To keep from skimming down onto the soft earth, he flap-flap-flapped his great wings to lift himself back into the sky. Because the earth was still soft, the wind from his wings made hills and valleys everywhere he passed as he climbed. As the earth dried, the hills and valleys hardened, so that we see them still.

Even with its hills and mountains, the bird and water animals were pleased with the new earth that rode upon the water. To keep it from sinking, the bird people tied each of its four corners to the rim of the sky dome with strong ropes.

The earth was finished, but there was still work to do. The new earth and its animals were living in the dark, for there was no light to see by. T-cho, the Sun, called a council to find someone to light the darkness. "Glow-worm can do it!" some cried, and so Glow-worm tried. He flew up and all around, but the glow he made came only in faint flickers. The people groaned.

"I can make light," said Yohah, the Star, and he climbed up the sky. Yohah's gleam was too dim to shine far.

"We need more!" the people called out.

Shar-pah, the Moon, stepped up and went to take a turn, but even she was too pale. The earth was lighter, but still too dark.

The people turned to the Sun. "Mother, what shall we do?"

T-cho, the Sun, smiled. "You are my children. I will make your light. I will shine for you." So she went off to the east to climb up into the sky. At her first step up, dawn broke. At her second, bright morning flooded over the earth. The earth's creatures sang out loud for joy as they watched her pass across the sky toward noon.

As T-cho passed over them, a drop of her blood fell to the ground, and from the blood and earth mixed together there sprang up the first human people, the Children of the Sun, the Yuchis.

THE CRYING PLACE

Caddo

In the days after the earth was shaped, the Caddo say, the old, magical animal people lived upon it, but the men and the animals we share the earth with now lived under it, shut up in darkness. In that time, humans and the everyday animals of all kinds were brothers and sisters. They lived in friendship, crowded together in the darkness, until one day one of their number discovered a way into a new cave, and saw a pinprick of light far ahead and far above.

"What is that?" the people cried when they peered into the new cave and saw it.

But no one knew. Old Man, their chief, sent a man to discover what it might be. "It is bright and shining air," that one said when he returned. "It falls down through a hole that opens into another world above."

The people and birds and beasts marveled at this news. They agreed at once that they would all of them climb up into the new world and leave the darkness behind. First went the Old Man, and then his wife. After them followed the other people. Their animal friends came walking and flying and hopping behind, and they all marveled, for even the dim light of the new cave was wonderful to them. Old Man, as he climbed, carried fire in a pipe in one hand and a drum in the other. His wife followed close behind. She carried with her corn in one hand and pumpkin seeds in the other. After Old Man and Old Woman, all the rest of the people and animals came climbing up through a hole in the ground into the bright, golden light.

As the people and deer and rabbits and possums and other animals came out of the hole, they went a little way off to wait for the others and to wonder at the shining new world. But Wolf, when he stepped up into the sunlight, said to himself, "Soon this new world will be as crowded as the darkness." And so he put his shoulder to a large rock above the mouth of the cave and pushed, and rolled it down into the hole. The rock carried more rocks with it, and closed the hole fast shut, and sealed all of the rest of the people and animals down in the darkness.

When Old Man and Old Woman and the people and animals discovered what Wolf had done, they sent up a great wail, and sat down on the ground and cried. Many of their friends, and many kinds of animals that we have never seen in this upper world, were lost to them. When they had no more tears to weep with, they named that hill

Cha'kani'na, the Place of Crying, and went down to the shore of the lake. From that place the animals went in all directions, and the people, who were the Caddo, began the long journey up the Red River into a land that they made their own. They carried with them the fire and the pipe and drum, and planted the corn and pumpkins where they made villages, and always called the ground out of which they had come *Ina',* their Mother.

FIRST WOMAN

Catawba

But the Catawba have a different tale of those days. When this world was still new, they say, all of it was sharp rocks and steep hills, high cliffs and jagged peaks—except for one small valley hidden deep in the mountains. There, it was always summer. A clear stream ran through its green meadows. The deer and the wolf drank from it side by side. Beavers built a dam to make a pond, and fishes swam in it. Flowers bloomed on the banks and did not die. Trees flowered and bore fruit, and then flowered again. Bluebirds and buntings sang in the branches. Bees hummed. Blackberries, raspberries, and gooseberries, huckleberries, serviceberries, and mulberries ripened all the year round. The little valley was the best of all places.

Once the Great Spirit had made the valley, he shaped a new creature to live in it. He made this new being to stand on two legs, much like himself. He gave it dark hair and eyes and a dress made of large round leaves of galax, and set her down in the grassy meadow.

"You are First Woman," said the Great Spirit, "and this is your home to live in and to rule." Then, when he had said it, he went away and left her.

First Woman was happy at first. She found a cave to shelter her from the always-summer rains, and made it her home. She ate berries with honey, and pawpaws and persimmons and fish. She swam with the beavers and ran with the deer, and neither she nor her valley grew old. Every day was the same as every other day, until she began to wish that it was not.

One day, as First Woman sat at the opening of her cave, she saw a bright red butterfly flutter by. She had never seen such a thing before, and so she rose and followed it. Down across the valley it flew, and up into a narrow ravine. First Woman climbed after it a long, winding way until it led her to the foot of a waterfall. But then it vanished. First Woman turned back, but took the wrong path, and wandered farther and farther out of her way. At nightfall, cold and weary and frightened, she curled up on the ground to sleep. A little before dawn she awoke to find a dark shape bending over her—not a wolf or panther, but a shape much like her own. Yet she was the only human being in this world.

"What are you?" she asked in fear. It was larger than she, its face fiercer. Its shirt and leggings were made of cloud, as if it had just stepped down from the sky.

The Sky Man reached down to help First Woman to her feet. "I was on my way from the evening star to the morning star," he said. "When I looked down, I saw first that you are very beautiful, and then that you were lost. I wish to help you find your way, and so I have come down to your world, even though the Great Spirit will be angered."

"Will He be?" First Woman asked fearfully.

"Yes," said the Sky Man, "for He has commanded that the People Above do not come down to this world unless He sends them. His anger is terrible, and I fear it." But he smiled at her. "Indeed, I would rather stay here with you than return to the World Above and His anger."

First Woman's heart filled with happiness, for she had been lonely and not known it. "Come," she said, and she took his hand and went with him down to her beautiful valley.

There they lived together as wife and husband, and in time First Woman bore a child. Only then did they begin to think of the times to come. First Woman knew that from their children and their children's children would come a people who would overflow the valley and fill the world. How would they live? The world outside was harsh and bare. Sky Man feared that their children would suffer even more because he had disobeyed the Great Spirit's command, and he was unhappy. Together, they prayed to the Great Spirit for his forgiveness.

In the World Above, the Great Spirit heard, and

knew that their hearts were good. He lifted his hand, and a great wind rose. He moved his hand, and the great wind pushed mountains closer together and made space for other valleys, and for prairies. And all this world was made beautiful.

When the work was done, the Great Spirit leaned down from the World Above and told First Woman and Sky Man that all this world was theirs. But he told them, too, that because Sky Man had disobeyed him, from that day they must work for their food. He told them that life would no longer be all summer. Now there would be winter, and with it bitter cold. He told them that there would come a time when they would see in the water of the beavers' lake that their hair had grown white. He told them that in time they must grow old, and die.

And First Woman and Sky Man looked at the beautiful world, and at their child, and still were glad.

THE GREAT FLOOD

Chitimacha

Long ago, the Chitimacha say, after the first making of this world, a great flood came upon the land. It drowned the trees and hills, and swallowed up the people who lived upon the earth. Wise men told of its coming, but only one man and one woman were wise enough to listen. This chief and his wife heard, and knew that it was useless to flee. In their country there were no high hills, and water can run faster than feet. So, since the wife was an excellent maker of pots, they began to make a huge clay pot. The people laughed and called them foolish.

No sooner was the pot made, and baked in the fire, than the rain began to pour, the river to rise, and the sea to swell. The chief and his wife climbed into their pot. "Come with us!" they called out, but the people did not listen. "Come with us!" they called out, but not even the animals listened. Only two rattlesnakes came. "We will come with you," the two snakes said, and they climbed in.

The four in the pot heard the rush of the wave as it came, and saw the swirl and foam of it as it swept over the village. The water lifted up the pot and swept it along, too. The pot bobbed along on top of the water until at last the rain stopped and the flood stood still. The chief and his wife and the two rattlesnakes looked out. They saw that there was no land left, and no sign of life. Even birds had drowned.

Only Red-headed Woodpecker and Ground Dove had escaped. As the waters rose, they flew all the way up to the sky dome and held on to the sky with their claws. *"Queeoh!"* and *"Woo-oo!"* they cried. *"Queeoh! Woo-oo!"* Red-headed Woodpecker was larger and his tail longer, and the water rose so high that part of his tail was covered. After that, and even now, the whole end of his tail is darker than the rest of it.

When at last the water went down a ways, still no land came in sight. When he saw this, the chief called the birds down to perch on the rim of the pot. "Woodpecker," he said, "fly out and find dry ground for us."

"Queeoh, I will," said Red-headed Woodpecker, and he went. He was gone for a very long time, and he came back weary and weak. "There is no earth to see," he said. After a while, when the water had gone down a little further, the chief said, "Ground Dove, fly out and find dry ground for us."

"Woo-oo, I will," Ground Dove said, and she went. She was gone for a very, very long time, but at last she came back with a single grain of sand in her beak.

The chief took the grain of sand and placed it on the water. At once the water there turned into dry land, and the sea drew away. The chief and his wife and the two rattlesnakes climbed out of the pot and traveled south over the new land to a place that became their new home. The children they had there became the Chitimacha people.

Because the chief and his wife had saved them, the two grateful rattlesnakes stayed in that country, too. It is said that if, in the old times, a Chitimacha family left its house for a time, a rattlesnake-friend moved in to keep watch over it. The rattlesnake bit or warned away any stranger who tried to come in, for he remembered that the Mother and Father of the Rattlesnakes owed their lives to the Mother and Father of the Chitimacha.

STONECOAT

Yamassee/Cherokee

As people began to spread out across this world, the Creator looked down and saw that there were many things they did not know. He saw that men hunted from morning to night, but often went home with no meat for their wives and children. He saw that women dug roots and gathered berries and picked fruit from dawn until dusk, and still they and their children felt hunger. He saw children and women and men suffer wounds in pain, and die from sicknesses when they could have been cured. So He called Ocasta, one of his helpers in the Above World, to Him.

"Ocasta," He said, "I have work for you. The people in the world below the sky live too hard a life. They do not know the best ways to hunt, or to fight their enemies. They do not know what medicine to use when they are sick. You must go down to their world and teach them all these things. Teach them, too, how to seek my help, for I wish them well."

"I will go," Ocasta said. "I will teach them."

And so Ocasta made his way down to this world, but his heart—which he had always hidden from the Creator—was full of anger. *I should be a great man in the Above World,* he thought. *Not a poor messenger to these little people.* The truth was that his heart held in it as much evil as it had goodness. He obeyed the Creator only because he was afraid of Him.

Ocasta's path down through the sky brought him to this world in the middle of the forest, and he set out to find a village. After a while he saw a man far ahead through the trees and quickly made himself invisible. That was his only real magic. He went closer and watched the man lift a long stick straight up in front of him, put a shorter stick across it, and point it at a deer. Next—somehow—the hunter pulled the long stick into a curve and sent the shorter one flying through the air. It struck the deer, and the deer fell down.

Ocasta had never seen such a thing as a bow and arrow. He stood closer to the deer than the man did, and so he ran to it and pulled out the flying stick. There, on the end that had killed the deer, was a sharp flint point.

Hai! thought Ocasta. "If this little stone point can kill such a large beast, perhaps it can kill me." He hated that the little people of this world could have such power over him. The anger in his heart swelled into rage. "We shall see," he said to himself, and he went on his way. Once he was out of sight of the hunter, he made himself visible again, and began to pick up pieces of flint. He stuck each piece to his long cloak as he went, until every bit of the cloak was covered. "Now I am safe," Ocasta said as he set off to find the nearest village. "And I shall teach these men what *I* wish."

When he came to the village he fastened his heavy cloak close around him and went from house to house, telling neighbors lies about neighbors and whispering bad thoughts into every ear. He taught old women spells for witchcraft and young men how to make cruel mischief. Soon every house was filled with troubles, and Ocasta was filled with delight.

Hai, I must find more people to teach! he thought happily, and so he set off toward the next village. As soon as he entered the woods, he made himself invisible so that no one would know where he went. Then when he had done his evil mischief in the next village, he did the same again, going in invisible spirit form from one place to another, always leaving trouble behind him.

The unhappy people soon began to say, "All of our troubles are this Stonecoat's fault. He must have power over us because he is more than a man. He knows many things we do not know. He has tricked and deceived us all. We must get rid of him, but how? We cannot shoot him. His cloak protects him." So they called together the wisest people in all their seven villages. The wise ones decided that to kill Ocasta they would have to follow his example, and trick him. They talked until far into the night, and at last hit upon a plan. Each village had at least one Bad Luck Woman who was such bad luck that a man who came near her was sure to fall ill, perhaps to die. The wise ones sent women messengers to these Bad Luck Women to ask their help.

The next day, Ocasta went on his way to the seventh and last village. The people knew which path the invisible Stonecoat had to take to get there, so they sent all of the Bad Luck Women to sit beside his path. Ocasta saw the first, and felt uneasy. An ordinary man would have fallen sick and dropped to his knees. Ocasta passed the second, and felt a little dizzy. An ordinary man would have moaned and rolled back and forth on the path. Past three, four, five Bad Luck Women, Ocasta staggered on. When he came to the seventh Bad Luck Woman, he fell down at last. As he fell, the last Bad Luck Woman jumped up and ran to pull back a piece of flint on his cloak so that she could drive a basswood stake through his heart.

The people of the seven villages gathered around, and when Ocasta spoke, they found to their surprise that the blow to his heart had let out all the wickedness.

"I will leave this world soon," Ocasta told them. "When I die you must burn my body on a fire of basswood, but until then you must listen." And he began to teach them all the things the Creator had sent him to teach. He taught them how to pray. He taught the songs for, and explained the steps of, the different hunting dances that would call up the bear or the deer or other animals. He taught songs and dances to help them defeat their enemies, and songs and dances and medicines to heal the sick. To some men he taught even more, and gave them great power, and these became medicine men.

At last Ocasta's strength was gone, and as his spirit left him, the people placed his body on the fire of basswood. His spirit began to sing, and rose up with the smoke to the World Above, singing. He had brought wickedness into the world, but in the end he brought great good, too.

The Coming of Corn

Choctaw

The Choctaw, like the Caddo, tell that their ancestors, the first Choctaws, came up out of the darkness. The place where they climbed out into the light was the sacred mound Nanih Waiya, by the creek that is now called Nanawaya. For many years the children of their children lived there by hunting and by eating the fruits and berries and roots of that land, and often they went hungry.

One day, a crow came flying across the Great Water from the south. He carried a single grain of corn in his beak as he flew over the great gulf. When he came to land, he flew on until he came to a village not far from Nanih Waiya. There were many people in the town, and the crow looked at each, but he flew on. At last he saw a small boy playing alone on the ground between the houses. The crow flew straight to the boy, and lit on the ground before him, and reached out and dropped the kernel of corn into his hand.

"I will call it *tauchi,*" the child said, and he thanked the crow. "I will plant it here," he said, and he planted the seed there in the open space between the houses.

The seed grew into a bright green sprout. The people stepped around it, and swept around it, but would not take care of it. Only the child, who was an orphan and owned nothing, thought it was beautiful. He dug around it to loosen the earth. He hilled up the earth around its stalk. He watered it. Its stalk grew, and sprouted leaves. It grew taller and bore two ears of corn. It ripened, and when the ears were opened and dried, the Choctaw people saw that the child had been wiser than they. So they ground the grains of the one ear into maize flour and saved the grains of the other for seed.

Each year after that they planted and grew *tauchi*.

And hunger became a stranger.

THE RABBIT WHO STOLE FIRE

Seminole

In the Early Time, the First People were not allowed to have fire for themselves, for fear some would give it to the people who lived across the great ocean water, or others. They did not have cookfires, or fires to warm their houses. Only when there was a dance did they have fire, for only on the dance ground could a fire be built. All the people kept watch there, to guard the Only Fire from each other.

One night the people of the town had a Stomp Dance, and for it they built a great fire. "Who shall we ask to lead the dance?" the firemakers asked. "Shall we ask Beaver, or Panther?"

"Let us ask Rabbit," said some. "He is the best singer, and makes a good dance leader, too."

So they agreed, and asked Rabbit to lead. He was happy to. At the dance, he sang the dance song and hopped and stomped around the fire circle in time with the drums. All the people joined in behind him. Rabbit led them in a wide circle, then suddenly danced up to the edge of the fire. There, to everyone's surprise, he gave a high hop and made strange signs in the air.

"*Hoh!* Wonderful! Rabbit, Rabbit, Rabbit!" the people cried in admiration.

Rabbit led the dance around a second time, this time in a wide circle of loops. He hopped and stomped in time to the drums, and after the last loop danced up to the fire again. Everyone stood back and cheered as he gave an even higher hop than before, and made even wilder signs in the air.

"*Hoh-hoh!* Wonderful! More, Rabbit, more!"

The third time around, the people stood back again to cheer as Rabbit danced toward the fire. But then suddenly he was not dancing. Instead he reached out, snatched a burning branch from the fire, and ran out into the darkness, toward the forest. For a moment the people stared after him in surprise. Then they all shouted and screamed and waved their fists, and chased after him. Rabbit was far ahead. He carried his branch like a torch and lit fires all the way through the woods so that people everywhere could come and take fire for themselves. Not one of the dancers from the Stomp Dance could run fast enough to catch him.

Because they could not catch Rabbit, the people all ran back to the dance ground to make rain medicine and dance for rain. When they did this, the rain came. It fell upon the forest and put out all of the fires. It put out Rabbit's torch, too.

When the rain stopped, the people moved into

a circle to start the Stomp Dance all over. Suddenly, there was Rabbit again, hopping and stomping at the head of the line, ready to lead. The dancers, when they saw him, began to shout.

"*Hoh!* Thief! How does Rabbit the Fire Thief dare to show his nose?"

"Stop him! He cannot lead the dance! He will try again to steal fire from us!"

"Surely not—besides, he is the best singer and dancer!"

"Throw him out on his ears!"

"Poh! What is a little fire? He cannot get far with it."

And so they began the Stomp Dance again with Rabbit leading as before. Once around, twice around, and everyone admired and cheered Rabbit's high steps and leaps and signs in the air even more than before. But then, just as before, he dashed to the fire and snatched up a firebrand. In a flash, he was gone and fires sprang up all along his path.

"Stop the tricky rascal!"

"After him, everyone!"

"Catch him! Stop him!" But no one was fast enough to catch Rabbit, so they returned to the dance ground. There, the wise men once again made rain medicine. Once again, rain poured down and put out all of Rabbit's fires.

"That takes care of Rabbit," the dancers said. "Let us begin again." And they moved into a circle, as before.

But Rabbit was not ready to give up. Too many people in the world needed fire. He started back to the dance ground, and on the way he passed by a big, hollow rock. He stopped, and looked inside.

"*Hoh!* Just what I need! No rain can reach me here," he said, and he put a little heap of firewood inside. Then he thought again. "It will be a very tight fit in there. What if my hair catches fire?" So he went looking for something to stick his hair down, and found some sap from a loblolly pine. It stuck his hair down nicely, and he set out for the dance ground as fast as he could run.

"Rabbit? Not again!" cried many of the dancers.

"How dare he?"

"Throw him out!"

But Rabbit's friends and those who admired his singing and dancing shouted, "Let him lead again! Why fear him?"

So Rabbit was chosen once more to lead the dance. This time he dashed straight to the fire, but as he bent over to pick up a burning branch, his hair burst into flames.

"Fire! Fire!" Rabbit shrieked in fright. He leaped into the air and ran for the forest faster than an arrow flies. His hair dropped sparks and set fires as he flew.

When he reached the hollow rock, he brushed the burning sap and hair from his head into the little heap of firewood and settled down to wait. The dancers had chased after him, but could not find him. When they went back to make rain medicine, the rain poured down but Rabbit and the fire stayed safely hidden.

As soon as the rain stopped, Rabbit slipped out and set fires in the trees and grass. The people at the Stomp Dance saw, and called up more rain to put them out. Three more times Rabbit tried, three more times it rained. When the people saw no more flames, they went home.

But Rabbit had a little bit of fire left. He crept out and carried it to the seaside, and swam with it to the island across the water. After a while Rabbit and the people across the water took it everywhere. In the daylight the Fire Keepers saw the smoke rising up in the distance and were angry, but there was nothing they could do.

And that is how fire came to everyone.

RABBIT'S HORSE

Creek

Rabbit wanted a wife, and so one morning he set out to look for one. On the way he met Wolf. "What a fine, bright day, Brother Wolf!" he called out quickly.

Wolf, whose belly was full, gave him a friendly nod. "So it is, Brother Rabbit."

Rabbit was so surprised by Wolf's friendly greeting that instead of hurrying past, he stopped to say, "Yes, and a fine day to go look for a wife. I am on my way to my neighbor's house to visit her handsome daughters. Why don't you come with me?"

"I think I will," said Wolf. "Come to think of it, I could use a wife, too."

So off they went, along the trail and up the hill and along the way, and came to the house of the old woman who was Rabbit's neighbor. Her two daughters invited them in. "Sit down," the girls said, and they sat down across from Rabbit and Wolf. Now, Wolf was a great talker, with a smooth tongue and fine tales of his adventures and travels. The girls laughed at his jokes, and listened to his stories with wide eyes. Rabbit was forgotten. He sat still for as long as he could bear to. Then he spoke up. "Brother Wolf," he said, "it is time to go home."

"So soon?" Wolf exclaimed. "How can you wish to leave? Let us stay just a little longer."

What could Rabbit do but smile and pretend to enjoy himself? It was evening, and Wolf's hunting hour, before he stood up to leave. Rabbit, on his way out, took the prettiest of the two girls aside to whisper to her so that Wolf would not hear. "I am pleased that you have enjoyed my visit," Rabbit said. "And it was good of you to be so kind to my old horse. You know he is my horse, of course."

"Your *horse?*" cried the girl. "I do not believe you!"

Rabbit looked hurt. "Do you think I would lie? Have you never seen me riding him?"

"No," said the girl. "And we won't believe it until we do."

"Very well, then," Rabbit said. "Tomorrow I will ride over, and you will see for yourself." He went out to join Wolf, and as they trotted down the path, the girls called after them, "Come again."

Early the next morning Wolf came to Rabbit's door. "Rabbit? Are you awake? Let us go visit the girls now!"

"Oh, Brother Wolf, I cannot," came Rabbit's answer. His voice was faint. "I was sick all night. My legs are too weak this morning to take me visiting. Perhaps tomorrow. Or the next day."

"Tomorrow?" Wolf yelped. "The next day? But, Rabbit, I cannot wait!"

"And I cannot walk," Rabbit replied in a small voice. "Unless, perhaps—"

"Yes?" Wolf said eagerly. "Perhaps—?"

"Perhaps if you would carry me on your back, I could go. The girls *are* very pretty," said Rabbit.

"Oh, Brother Rabbit, of course I will carry you!" Wolf said.

So Rabbit climbed from his bed onto Wolf's back, and they set off along the trail. When they came to the hill, Rabbit fell off.

"Ow, ow, ow!" moaned Rabbit. "Your fur is not long enough to hold on to, and I am so weak. But—but perhaps if I had a bridle?"

"Very well," said Wolf, and he went back to find a bridle. He put it on when he returned, and Rabbit climbed up on Wolf's back once again. Off they went, but on the way down the other side of the hill, Rabbit fell off a second time.

"Oh, oh, oh!" he squeaked. "My legs are too shaky to hold on to your sides. But—but perhaps if you tied some sandburs to my heels they would hold fast to your fur."

"Like spurs?" Wolf frowned. "No, no, I am too ticklish."

"Oh, no, I will not spur you with them. My legs are too weak for that," said Rabbit. "Just before we come to the girls' house, we will take off the bridle and burrs, and I will do my best to walk."

"Very well," Wolf agreed, so they tied on the burrs and traveled on. Then, suddenly, when they were only a short distance from the girls' house, Rabbit lifted up his heels and stuck his spurs hard into Wolf's sides. Wolf gave a mighty yelp of *"OW!"* and took off past the house at the speed of an arrow.

The two girls watched from their doorway as Rabbit and Wolf raced on by. Wolf did not stop until the edge of the woods beyond. There Rabbit tied him—still panting, "Ow, ow, ow!"—to a post. Then he walked back to the girls.

"There, you see!" said Rabbit. "I told the truth."

"You did," they said. "And what a fine horse he is!" So they invited Rabbit in, and that same day the prettier sister agreed to be his wife.

Wolf at last pulled free of the post. "Gr-r-row! That Rabbit will never trick me again," he vowed. And Rabbit did not.

Until the next time.

RABBIT AND WILDCAT

Natchez

One morning Rabbit trotted along a forest path, thinking about this and that—and suddenly there was Wildcat. Terrible Wildcat! Wildcat who ate rabbits.

"Heh, heh! Good morning, friend Wildcat. I am so glad I found you," Rabbit wheezed. He hopped up and down in fright. "It is s-such good luck. A little way b-back I passed a flock of beautiful fat turkeys. I am no turkey eater, but it seemed a shame to let them go to waste. And then I thought of you."

Wildcat's whiskers twitched. Juicy, dark turkey meat would make a tasty breakfast, but here was Rabbit, right underfoot. Wildcat stepped closer. "I do not know," he said. "Turkeys are easily frightened. They can run almost as fast as they fly. Hunting them is hard work."

Rabbit hopped backward. "Oh, yes, yes, you're right. You are, you are. But I know of a way you can catch one or two without running a step."

Wildcat liked the sound of that. "Tell me," he said.

"Certainly. Yes, indeed. All you have to do is lie down here and pretend to be dead. Then I will hurry off to tell the turkeys that their old enemy is dead, and bring them to see."

Wildcat liked the sound of that. After all, he was hungry enough to eat a turkey or two and Rabbit, as well. "Very good," he said, and he lay down in a wide place in the trail.

Rabbit hopped over to a fallen tree trunk nearby and brought some crumbly pale rotten wood dust to smear around Wildcat's mouth and eyes, and dusty earth to rub into his fur. "There! You look as if you've been dead for days," he said. "Do not move," he called as he hurried away.

The turkeys were still where he had seen them, scratching for seeds and grubs. "Oh, friends!" he cried, hopping up and down. "Wonderful news! Our old enemy Wildcat is dead. It is true! I have seen him. He lies stiff as a log on the path up ahead. Old Wildcat is dead!"

The turkeys gobbled in excitement. "Wildcat is dead! Wildcat is dead!"

"Come see, come see," Rabbit cried. "I am so happy that I feel like singing. Let us all celebrate. Come dance a dance of thanksgiving around him, and I will sing of our good luck."

The turkeys gobbled in glee and bustled after Rabbit, eager to see the last of their old enemy. When they came upon his body stretched across the path, they gobbled with laughter. His mouth was wide open, and his feet stiff in the air. "Come, dance," Rabbit urged. "Dance!" Then, as the turkeys

danced, he began to sing. *"Old Wildcat is dead,"* he sang. *"The old biter is dead, so dance, hoh, hoh! Teeth can't bite, claws can't scratch, hoh, hoh! Snatch that redheaded one, catch that fat one, so dance, hoh, hoh!"*

The turkeys stopped dancing. "What kind of song is that to be singing? Snatch us and catch us?"

"What is wrong with that?" Rabbit asked quickly. "I was just singing about his old wickedness. That is over, so let us all dance! *Teeth can't bite, claws can't scratch!"* he sang, and to prove it, he jumped on Wildcat's body. *"We dance on you, old Biter, we stomp on you,"* he sang.

The turkeys followed him, dancing *step-stomp-step* over Wildcat's body. Wildcat waited until the fat, redheaded one danced onto his chest, and caught him, *snap!* As he gobbled him up, the rest of the turkeys squawked in terror, scrabbled away, and scattered through the trees.

Rabbit did not wait for Wildcat's thanks. He was already gone.

HOW RABBIT STOLE OTTER'S COAT

Cherokee

In the First Time, just as now, the animals wore fur or skin coats of different colors, different patterns and designs. Some were of long fur, some of short, some silky and some coarse. There were brown coats and black, red ones and yellow, plain and striped and spotted. But no one could agree whose coat was the most handsome. Bear growled that it was his. Deer said that it was Fawn's. Other animals claimed that their own coats were shiniest or warmest or best-fitting. "Mine is softest," Mole piped up. They argued until at last they grew weary of arguing. "Let us hold a council of all the animals," they said, "and let them decide for us. They will probably say that Otter's is finest of all."

"Hoh!" Rabbit scoffed. "As fine as mine? Have you ever seen Otter's? I haven't. He lives so far up the creek that he never comes down to visit. What is it like, this coat of his?"

It was so long since anyone had seen Otter that no one could remember what his coat looked like, only that it was a handsome one. They did not even know how far up the creek he lived. "But when he hears about the council, he will come," they said.

Everywhere that Rabbit went that day, he heard the animals talk of Otter's handsome coat, and he began to worry. He began to think how he might trick Otter out of his fine coat. First, he asked sly questions of a few of the older animals. None knew how far up the creek Otter lived, but some did remember the path by which he always came down to the council place.

Rabbit hopped off at once along that trail. He traveled for three days and met no one, but on the fourth day he saw a fellow in a beautiful, silky, dark brown fur coat walking toward him.

"Good morning, stranger!" the fellow called. "I am Otter. Who are you, and where are you going this good morning? The council meeting is back the way you have come."

"I am Rabbit," Rabbit said. "I have been sent to bring you to the council house. It is a long time since you have made the journey there. The animals feared that you might have forgotten the road."

"No, not at all," Otter said, "but I am glad to have company on the way." So they went along together.

That night Rabbit chose their camping place, and cut bushes to heap up for beds. The next day as they went along, he picked up sticks of wood. Soon he was carrying a large load of firewood on his back, and Otter asked why.

"Oh," Rabbit said, "to be sure that we have enough at our camp tonight to keep us warm."

Just before sunset they stopped and made camp. After their meal Rabbit began to whittle on a stick of wood. "That looks like a paddle," said Otter. "What do you need a paddle for? We have no canoe to paddle down the creek."

"Oh," Rabbit said, "it is to sleep on. I always have good dreams when I sleep with my head on a paddle."

When he finished his whittling, once again Rabbit cut bushes for beds, but after their beds were made, he kept on cutting bushes. Otter watched as he cut a path all the way down to the water, and thought it very strange. "Why do you do that?" he asked.

"Oh," said Rabbit, "because this is The Place Where It Rains Fire. Sometimes it happens, and tonight the sky looks angry. I will keep watch while you sleep. If fire starts to fall, I'll give a shout. If you hear me call, you must run to the stream and jump in. Perhaps, to be safe, you should hang your coat on a limb of the sour gum tree yonder, so it won't be burned."

Otter shivered and said, "Thank you, friend Rabbit, I shall!"

With Otter's coat hung up safely under the sour gum tree, Rabbit and Otter curled up on their beds of brushwood. Rabbit only pretended to sleep. He stayed awake and waited until the fire burned down to red coals.

"Otter?" he whispered.

Otter was fast asleep, and did not twitch. After a little while Rabbit called out more loudly, "Otter!" When Otter did not move, Rabbit crept to the fire with his paddle and used it to scoop up a heap of hot coals. With a shout, he threw the coals straight up into the air and cried out, "Fire, fire! The sky is raining fire!"

Otter leaped up as hot coals fell all around him. "The water!" Rabbit shouted. "Run for the water!"

Otter raced down to the stream and jumped in. He was so badly frightened that ever since then he has thought it safer to live close to or in the water. Rabbit, of course, snatched Otter's coat from the tree branch, left his own in its place, and went happily on his way.

At the council place, all of the animals had gathered, and everyone was waiting and watching for Otter. They had saved the best seat for him. At last someone called out, "He is coming! Otter is coming!" Squirrel was sent out to meet the famous Otter and take him to his seat. The rest lined up to welcome him one by one. "Otter" kept his head bowed down and a paw over his face, and each animal who gave him greeting wondered why he was so bashful. But no one asked until Bear stepped up.

"What's this?" roared Bear.

He reached out and pulled "Otter's" paw away. There sat Rabbit with his rabbity split nose. Rabbit hopped up and sprang over the bench and away, but not before Bear gave a great swipe with one paw and clawed off all but a stub of Rabbit's tail.

Rabbit must have left Otter's coat behind, too, for Otter is wearing a fine one still.

HOW ALLIGATOR'S NOSE WAS BROKEN

Seminole

The animals loved a good ball game, so one time when they all were gathered together, they decided to dare the birds to play against them. Alligator was elected chief of the animal side. At once he sent deer off at a dash to challenge the birds. The birds sent up a cheer, for they loved a good ball game, too. They elected Eagle to lead their side, and sent Heron flapping back to the animals' camp to accept the challenge. It was agreed that they would meet in three days to play the game.

For the rest of the day Alligator and the animals, and Eagle and the birds, made plans. First each side chose their players, the fastest and strongest and cleverest. Then the chiefs met to choose a playing ground. When the field was chosen, they measured the distance from the center of the ground to the place for the animals' goal and, on the other side, for the birds' goal. Two tall poles were planted to mark each goal. Next, the animal medicine man and bird medicine man cast conjure spells on the balls. Each side hoped its medicine man's magic was the stronger.

On the day of the ball game, the two teams—

forty animals and forty birds—set off for the ball ground. As they came near, each side sang its war song, and shouted its war shout. Then the animals, painted with red as if for war, and dressed up with feathers in their fur, ran onto the field at full trot. The birds flew in at full flap, painted with red and dressed up with tufts of fur on their heads. Each side ran in circles around its own goal poles, the animals barking and roaring, the birds cackling and screaming. Around the field, their wives and children and old mothers and fathers cheered and made bets that their own side would win.

Then the game chiefs called for quiet. The ball was tossed in the air, and the game began.

Back and forth and forth and back it went, all afternoon, but no one made a goal. Then, just as the ball flew overhead toward the birds' poles, Alligator leaped up with a push from his great tail, opened up his great jaws, and snatched it out of the air. Holding it in his teeth, he ran for the far end of the ball ground.

The animals squeaked and barked and roared, "Go! Go! Go!" Alligator's wife ran alongside the ball ground and shouted, "Look, look at Little Striped Alligator's daddy! Oh, see him go, see him go!" The animals jumped up and down in triumph.

But just then Eagle, who was circling high above the field, folded his wings and dropped. He fell like a sharp, feathered rock, and struck Alligator so hard on his nose that he broke it.

"*Ai-yi!*" bellowed Alligator, and he opened his mouth wide.

In a flash, Turkey poked his head in among Alligator's long, sharp teeth, pulled out the ball, and ran. He reached the birds' goal, threw the ball between the poles, and won the game for the birds.

And ever since that day, Alligator has had a sunken place on his snout where Eagle broke it.

HERON AND HUMMINGBIRD

Hitchiti

One day Heron and Hummingbird decided to race each other. Indeed, all of the animals and birds loved nothing better than daring each other to a race (unless it was playing in a ball game). "Let us race from here to the big dead tree that stands on the bank of the wide river four days toward the sunset," Heron said to Hummingbird.

"Agreed!" answered Hummingbird. "And whoever lights on the tree first will own the right to the water and all the fish in it!"

"Agreed!" Heron squawked happily. "I shall win easily," he bragged. "My wings are as much wider than yours as the deer's legs are longer than the mouse's."

"Hah!" scoffed Hummingbird. "For every flap of your wings, mine beat many, many times. I can fly too fast for you to see."

"We will see about that! Shall we set off at dawn tomorrow?"

Hummingbird hesitated. "Dawn comes very early. Let us start at midday instead."

So they did. When the sun was at its highest the next day, the two birds met. Long-legged Heron drew

a line in the earth and stood behind it, Hummingbird hovered beside him, and together they cried, "Go!" Heron gave a great beat of his wings and rose into the air, then flapped away west toward the far-off river. Hummingbird zipped along until he was far ahead, then stopped to sip from the blossoms of a flowering honeysuckle bush. While he was tasting their nectar, Heron flew past high overhead, *flap-flap-flap*. When Hummingbird was finished sipping from the flowers, he whizzed on and soon passed Heron. When he was miles ahead, he stopped in a meadow fringed with milkweed to taste a dozen or two. While he flitted from one flower head to the next, Heron passed overhead and flew steadily on— but it was not long before Hummingbird zipped ahead once again.

All day it went like this, but at night Hummingbird stopped to perch for the night, and sleep. Heron flew on. By dawn he was far ahead, but then Hummingbird awoke and whizzed along so fast that he passed Heron once again. The rest of the day went just as the day before had gone. At nightfall Hummingbird stopped again and slept until dawn while Heron traveled all night. When morning came, Hummingbird chased after him again and passed him. The third night and the fourth were the same.

On the fourth morning Hummingbird rose with the sun and zipped along happily, but when he came to the place where the dead tree stood on the bank of the great river, Heron was already there, sitting on its one dead branch.

"I see you, friend Hummingbird," Heron called happily. "Don't forget what we agreed. We said that whichever of us perched here first would win the right to all the water and the fish who live in it. The water is all mine, now! No drinking allowed."

At first Hummingbird was too angry and surprised at losing to answer. Then, "Poh!" he said haughtily. "Who needs water?"

And ever since that day he has drunk only the sweet nectar of flowers.

BIGFOOT BIRD

Eastern Cherokee

No'ghwisi, the bird called Meadowlark, lives in the lowlands, and he is about the same size as Quail. He walks the same way that Quail walks. Once, long ago, one meadowlark had feet that did not stop growing when the rest of him did. His feet grew stronger and stronger, his toes longer and longer, and his heart heavier and heavier.

"Poor feet, you are so ugly!" good Meadowlark cried. "And so heavy! When I try to soar up to the sky, you weigh me down. How can I sing my beautiful song if I cannot soar? If I do sing, the animals and other birds will not hear, for they will be too busy laughing. Oh, feet! I wish I were a mole and could hide under the earth!" Instead, Meadowlark hid in the grass and tried not to look at his feet. He hunted insects there and built his nest there. Sometimes he sang his beautiful song softly to himself there.

One day, Grasshopper came looking for Meadowlark. As he hopped through the grass he heard the soft little song and followed it to the downhearted bird. "Why are you hiding, friend Meadowlark?" he asked when he found him. "No one has seen you all summer."

Meadowlark hung his head. "I am ashamed to show my beak," he said.

"But why?" Grasshopper cocked his own head in puzzlement.

"Can't you see?" the bird asked with a sigh. He held up one long foot. "Because my feet are so long."

Grasshopper shrugged. "So? Why worry? One of these days they'll turn out to be useful."

Meadowlark blinked. "Useful? How?"

"How should I know? They will. You'll see," said Grasshopper. "You want to sing, don't you? Well, stop this hiding-in-the-grass nonsense and go out and do it."

Grasshopper's visit cheered Meadowlark so much that he went out then and there to take to the air. He flew low over the fields, and the trills and rills of his silver song soared high. All of the animals stopped still to listen to it. All of the birds folded their wings and perched in the trees to listen to it. On the following day Meadowlark went out again to sing, but as he flew, his toes now and then skimmed the feathery seed tops of grass. He could not help thinking, *Oh, how long my poor feet are, and how ugly!* With a sob, he dropped to the ground and hid again.

Not far away was a wheat field near a Cherokee town. A little female bird had made her nest in the middle of the wheat field. She had laid her eggs there, but now the wheat was ripe, and she heard men saying that it was time to cut it. "Oh, what shall I do? What shall I do?" she cried as she huddled over her eggs. She wept and wailed loudly, for she had no way to save them.

Grasshopper heard her cries, and followed them to her nest. "Why do you cry?" he asked.

"Who would not cry?" she wailed. "Men are going to cut the wheat. My eggs will be broken and crushed, for I have no way to carry them to safety."

"Well, now," said Grasshopper, "I know a bird over in the meadow beyond your field who is always hiding because his feet are so big. He could help you."

The little bird hopped off her nest. "I shall go see him at once. Perhaps he can pick up and carry my eggs in his claws."

She flew off in a flutter to find Meadowlark, who said, "Of course I will help, if I can."

Meadowlark followed her back to the wheat field, and found that with his long toes it was easy to pick up her eggs. Two at a time, he carried them off to the meadow grass and set them down in a safe nesting place. "That Grasshopper is a wise little fellow," he said happily.

And he flew up to circle the meadow and sing his beautiful meadowlark song.

Opossum and Her Children

Koasati

Opossum was always chasing after her six children. The little opossums loved to follow their noses and got lost at least four times a day. If Opossum left all six at home to go searching for food, only four were there when she returned. She had to go snuffling through the meadow grass to find the other two. If she went to sleep with six, she woke up with two, and had to dash out of her den to find the other four. One evening as she called them to her and caught one, Big Bat swooped down and scooped up two. "Ee-ee-eee!" squealed Opossum. She shooed a second child into their den, but as she did so, Big Bat returned and snatched two more. "My children! My children!" Opossum cried. The two little opossums in the den came back out to see what all the noise was, and Big Bat flew down and carried them off, too.

"My children! My children!" Opossum wailed, and she scuttled after them as fast as her short legs could run. From far off she saw Big Bat and her little ones disappear into an opening in the rocks.

"Oh, oh! My children, my children!" she cried as she ran around in circles. "What shall I do? What shall I do?"

Wolf was passing by and heard her cries, and came running. "What is wrong? What has happened? Why are you crying?"

"Oh, Wolf! Something big and dark, with wings, has flown off with all my children. It has stolen them and carried them into a hole in the hill!"

"Hoh!" said Wolf. "Show me the place. I will go there and bring your children back to you."

Opossum ran as fast as she could to the rocky hill, with Wolf close at her heels. When they came to the hole in the rocks, Wolf said, "Stay here!" and trotted inside. Almost at once he gave a loud yelp. "Ai-*yeek!*" he cried, and then, *"Hoh! Hoh! Hoh!"* and he scrambled backward out of the hole. "I can't do it. I can't do it!" he whimpered, and limped off with his tail between his legs.

"Oh, oh! My children, my children!" cried Opossum, and she ran off weeping and squeaking, "Oh! Oh!"

In a little while Rabbit came hopping along, and stopped. "What is wrong? Why are you crying? What has happened?" he asked.

"Oh, Rabbit!" she cried. "Something dark and big with wings has flown off with all my children. It has stolen them and carried them into a hole in the rocks!"

"Ah!" said Rabbit. "Where is this place? Take me there."

So Opossum ran back toward the hill as fast as

her legs would take her, and Rabbit hopped along at her side. When he saw the opening in the hill, he said, "Wait here," and dashed in. He had gone only a little way when Opossum heard him squeal, *"Eeeeek!"* and thump loudly with his feet. He bounded out of the hole, crying, "I cannot, I cannot!" and staggered away.

"My children, my children! Oh, oh," Opossum sobbed, and she ran around in circles crying and yelping, "Oh! Oh!" When Highland Terrapin came along, he stopped when he saw her. "Why are you crying? What has happened? What is wrong?"

"Oh, Terrapin!" Opossum cried. "A big, dark thing with wings flew off with all my children and carried them into a deep, dark hole!"

"What hole?" asked Highland Terrapin.

Opossum pointed. "There, in the hill," she said, still weeping.

Highland Terrapin lowered his head and walked in. The hole was very dark, and hot, but he could hear the little opossums squeak, so he went on. "I come," he called to them, but then he cried out, *"Ai-he-he-ho!"* as his first foot stepped on hot coals.

Still, he kept going, over the coals. He picked up the little opossums, put them on his back, and staggered across the hot coals and out. As soon as he was gone, Big Bat fluttered out and away.

"My children!" Opossum cried as she ran to

meet Highland Terrapin, but he held up a foot to stop her.

"From now on you must keep your children safe," he said. With one claw he drew a line across her belly, and suddenly she had a pocket there. "When they are little you must keep them inside. When they are bigger you must carry them on your back as I do."

So he put them up on her hips, and that is where opossums have carried their bigger-than-little children ever since.

FOX AND CRAWFISH

Natchez

Fox was trotting along the riverbank and saw Crawfish walking along ahead of him. Fox had not eaten since morning, so he licked his lips and said to himself, "*Hai!* A little taste of crawfish would do me nicely until dinnertime."

He crept ahead silently, his mouth open and ready to snap, but just as he was about to pounce, Crawfish turned and saw him.

"I s-see you!" Crawfish called out in surprise and fear. He swung around and raised his claws ready to pinch Fox's nose.

Now, "I see you" was also the polite way to greet a friend or visitor, so Fox quickly put on his best smile and gave a polite reply. "I am here. Are you well, friend Crawfish?"

"Well enough," said Crawfish. "Come, put away your smile, Fox. I know you mean to eat me. You are big enough and strong enough to do it, but do not try unless you want a sore nose."

Fox hesitated. He was very fond of his nose. It was a sharp, neat little nose, and an excellent sniffer. But he *was* very hungry.

Crawfish saw Fox's hungry look, and said quickly,

"All right, how about this? We run a race. If you can beat me to the finish, you can eat me. If *I* win, you don't."

Fox was delighted, for he was sure that he could outrun an awkward little fellow like Crawfish. When Crawfish suggested that the race be run over the seven hills to the west, and that the finish mark would be the stream beyond the seventh hill, Fox agreed, and drew a line in the earth for their starting point. Fox's tail twitched in excitement as they crouched down together behind the line, and he stared eagerly ahead. Crawfish swiveled one eye around as Fox's tail come to rest beside him, and reached out a claw to clamp on to it.

"Let's go!" he shouted.

Fox sprang away in a flash of red fur, with little Crawfish flying along at his tail. He was so small that Fox could not feel him there. Over one hill, two, three, four—Fox was panting as he raced up and over the seventh hill. When he reached the bottom of the hill, he whirled around to see whether Crawfish was coming. Not a claw in sight! But—as Fox whirled, his tail whisked around and Crawfish was thrown on ahead.

Fox turned to trot on to the river finish line, and stopped, for there was Crawfish, waving a claw to greet him.

"I knew that you could never run fast enough!" called Crawfish. And he jumped into the river.

HOW THE BITERS AND STINGERS GOT THEIR POISON

Choctaw

Long ago, when the Choctaw people first came up out of the earth into this world, a dangerous vine grew in the shallow water at the edges of the bayous. It was strong and green and handsome, but full of poison. When the people swam in the bayou, or went into the water to bathe, the vine was always there just under the water or close by. Often they brushed against it, or touched it. Sometimes they took hold of it in mistake for some other vine. When this happened, the poison entered them and made them ill. Many people drowned, or died of poison sickness.

The poor vine was miserable, for it had a kind heart, and meant no harm. It liked the Choctaw people, and was unhappy when it saw their pain and the sorrow of their families. But what could it do? It had no way to warn the little children. It could not wriggle out of the way when the big boys and girls swam too near. It could not pull its roots free and drift away when the women came to wash their pots or fetch water. It could do nothing when the men dipped their hands instead of their nets into the water for crawfish. The people fell sick, their families wailed in fear, and the vine grew still more unhappy.

"I must *do* something," it moaned to itself. "I must think how to get rid of my poison!"

The vine thought for three days, and then asked the Bald Cypress Tree to call the chiefs of the snakes and spiders, bees and wasps, mosquitoes, and all of the other bad-tempered creatures to a meeting beside the bayou. These sour-hearted animals had heard tales of the poison vine. They were all curious, and so they came. The snakes gathered at the water's edge, the insects settled out of their reach on the cypress trees' knees, and everyone listened to what the vine had to say.

"I am weary," it said, "of being an enemy of men. I wish to be their friend. You, my friends, often wish to be their enemies. I have decided to give all of my poison to whichever of you would like to have it, for I want none of it."

Now, in those days, none of the animal or insect people had poison to use with their fangs or stingers. A few of the snakes thought it a bad idea, but others, and almost all of the insects, were excited. "It could be useful to punish men for coming too close to us," some said.

"I'll take it!" all of them cried all at once.

So they talked and argued among themselves,

and after many harsh words and much buzzing, they came to an agreement. They would share the vine's poison among them.

Rattlesnake spoke up first. "I sshall take a ssshare, but I sshall be fair to man. I sshall warn him before I ssstrike by rattling my tail. If he iss too foolissh to listen and turn away, I sshall ssstrike."

Water Moccasin spoke up next. "I, too, will take a sshare of your poison, but I am no enemy to man. I sshall bite him only if he ssteps on me."

Small Ground Rattler was the most excited of all. "Hoh, yesss! I will be pleased to have ssome of your poison. When I have it, I will jump at men and bite them whenever I can!"

And he has done just that ever since.

But the vine is happy because since then he has poisoned no one at all.

Why the Buzzard Is Bald

Biloxi

Once, in the Old Days long, long ago, a man was walking home from fishing. Not far from one village he passed by a house that stood by itself, and heard a woman crying. *"Oh-oh, oh!"* the woman wailed as she wept. It was a fine, bright day, but the door of the house was shut and the window openings and the smoke hole were covered. *"Oh-oh, oh-h!"* the woman sobbed.

This is very strange, thought the man. So when he saw a crack in the wall of the house, he put his eye to the crack and looked in.

The room inside was full of shadows, but he saw the woman where she sat on a floor mat. She rocked back and forth as she sobbed and sighed, and she cried again and again, *"Oh-oh, oh-h-h!"*

The man watched and listened for a little while. Then he called out, "Open the door."

The woman did not seem to hear, but went on rocking and wailing. *"Oh-oh, oh-h-h-h!"*

"Open the door!" the man called again.

When she did not, he closed his eyes and said to himself, "I am as small as an ant. I look just like an ant. I am an ant."

As soon as he spoke the words, it was so. The man was gone, and a small red ant stood outside the door. With a wave of its feelers, the ant walked through the crack under it.

On the other side, the small red ant said to himself, "I am a man." As soon as he spoke it, it was so, and he was.

The man sat down facing the woman and spoke to her kindly. "You are beautiful. Why do you sit here in the shadows and cry?"

The woman trembled. "Because night will come, and I am afraid. Every night a strange monster flies down from the sky. When it walks on the earth, it snatches up people and eats them, and tonight it will eat me. I know that it will!"

"Where does this monster land when it comes down to earth?" the man asked. "Show me the place."

The woman saw that the man was no ordinary man. "I will," she said, even though she was still afraid. So she rose and went out of her house, and led him to a clearing in the forest.

"Good," the man said. "Now go home, for the sun is setting, and darkness grows in the grass and under the trees."

So she went, and when she was gone the man lay down in an open place to wait. When night came, so did the monster. A huge shape swooped down on the man with a terrible scream, but he leaped up with his knife in his hand, and fought it, and killed it.

"*Hoh!* You are an ugly thing!" the man exclaimed. With his knife he cut off the monster's snout, and an ear. He put them in his pouch, and set out once more for home.

Soon after sunrise the next morning, the Old Man of all the Black-headed Buzzard people flew by, and smelled the dead monster. He came down to look. "Hah!" said he as he walked all around the horrible thing. "This must be the creature who has killed so many people in this place. They will reward the monster killer well, I think." And then he cackled, for he had had an idea.

First the Old Man of the Black-headed Buzzards cut off the monster's other ear and a bit of its hide. Then he went to the center of the village nearby, and called out. "I have killed the monster! The monster is dead! Come and see!"

All of the people came out of their houses, and followed the Old Man of the Black-headed Buzzards to the house of their chief. "Here is the great monster killer!" they cried. "Let us make him a chief, too!"

When their own chief came out, the Old Man of the Black-headed Buzzards showed him the monster's ear and the bit of hide. "You have done well," said the chief, "and it shall be as the people wish. You shall be my brother-chief."

At that, the people brought water to wash the Old Man of the Black-headed Buzzards clean, for his kind are dirty birds, and they stink. When he was clean and sweet-smelling, they took him to the place where the chief's seat sat on a raised mound, and gave him a seat beside it. But before they could name him chief, the woman who had met the real monster killer cried out, "The bird lies! It was not he who saved us."

The people listened to the woman's story, and then sent runners to look for the man she told of. When they found him, he came with them to the village and threw the monster's snout and first ear to the ground before the chief's seat.

He pointed to the Old Man of the Black-headed Buzzards with scorn. "Have you made this liar a chief, then? Here is what I think of him!" And he snatched up Old Man Buzzard and thrust his head into the fire, and threw him to the ground.

The Old Man of the Black-headed Buzzards did not say a word. He could only make the kind of blowing noise that buzzards still make today, and his head was burned bald. He fled in shame.

And as a reward, the true monster killer won the beautiful woman for his wife.

The Girl Who Married a Star

Caddo

One summer night a Caddo girl took her sleeping mat out into the warm darkness to sleep under the wide sky. As she waited for sleep, she watched the stars sparkle against the darkness. One seemed to her to be more beautiful and to sparkle more brightly than the others.

"Oh, Star," she whispered, "I wish you could become a man and marry me. There is not even one young man in our village whom I like. Oh, Star, be a man, and marry me!"

The girl fell asleep in the middle of wishing, and when she awoke the stars were gone and she was in a strange place. She looked around her and saw a fire burning in a fire pit, and a strange old man sitting beside it. An old woman was stirring food in a stew pot. The girl sat up, afraid.

"Where am I? Who are you?" she asked.

The old man smiled. "You have your wish. You are at home above the Sky Dome. I am the Star, and you are now my wife."

The girl began to weep, for the old man was wrinkled and homely. She was young and strong and beautiful, and when she dreamed of a husband, her dream-husband was young and strong and beautiful, too. The old woman, who was the Star's sister, smiled at her kindly. "Don't cry," she said. "Come and eat."

The girl decided that she must make the best of things, and so she dried her tears and went to eat. Afterward, the old woman took her out to dig potatoes for their next meal. The girl dug for a while, but then came to a place where a giant potato lay half buried. It was twice as large around the middle as she was.

"Star Sister, what is this? What is this great potato for?"

"Ah," said the Star's sister. "That is the door of heaven. It hides the opening that leads from this Land Above the Sky Dome down to the world you came from."

"Oh, oh!" cried the girl, and she began to weep again. "Oh, how I wish I were down there! Please, won't you let me go home to my own people? I am so unhappy here. My husband is not the husband I thought I was wishing for. Oh, I wish I had not wished!"

The Star's sister took her back to their home and told her brother everything that his new wife had said. "Ah," he sighed. "Very well. In six days you may return to your home. It will take you that long to make ready, for you must make the rope on which you will climb down."

"I will help her," said Star Sister, and they went out to strip bark from young elm trees to braid into a rope to take the girl back down to earth. Old Man Star helped, too, but when the sixth day came, the rope was barely half long enough. It took five days longer. On the day that it was finished, Star Sister made corn cakes for the girl to eat on the long journey down, and filled a gourd with water to drink.

"You must start at dawn tomorrow," said the Star, "for you have a long way to go. The journey to earth will take you ten winters and summers."

The next morning they went together to the great potato. The Star and his sister tied the end of the rope around the girl's waist, then lifted up the potato and lowered her down through the hole. At first she saw only the dark sky, but after a while she saw the earth far, far below. As the rope was lowered down, down, down, the air that had been warm grew cold, then warm again, then cold, and the girl knew that summers and winters were going by on the earth below. At last her food was almost gone, but she was still far above the earth. And then she stopped. The rope would go no farther. She hung there and swung back and forth. When she had eaten the last of her food and drunk the last of her water, she grew hungry and weary. At the very last, she looked down and saw Buzzard circling below her.

"Oh, Brother Buzzard!" she cried. "Help me, help me!"

Buzzard was so surprised to see a girl hanging in the sky that he flew up to her at once. When he heard the tale of her troubles, he told her to climb onto his back. "I will fly you down the rest of the way to earth," said he.

Buzzard flew down and down and down. The earth came nearer and nearer. But the girl was heavy, and Buzzard grew weary. When he saw Hawk flying below, Buzzard croaked, "Help, Hawk! Help me carry Star's wife to earth!"

Hawk flew up to them, and took the girl on his back, and flew on down toward the earth. But the girl was heavy, and Hawk was even smaller than Buzzard. He flew on until they could see the mountains and rivers on the world below but then he, too, grew weary. Buzzard was following, and saw this. "Fly close, and I will carry her the rest of the way," he said. And he did.

When they reached the earth, Buzzard skimmed across the treetops and set the girl down at the edge of the forest near her own village. "There is the lodge where your parents live. Go straight there. Do not let anyone but your mother and father see you yet."

The girl was so weak that she went very slowly. Halfway home she met her mother, who did not know her, for she was so thin and so changed. When the girl said, "Mother, it is I," she threw her arms around her, and took her home. There she nursed her until the tenth day, when she was well enough to greet all of the people. When they came to welcome her back, the girl told them of her foolish wish and her journey, and of the great kindness of Buzzard.

And from that time on, when the Caddo people went out on a buffalo hunt, they always killed and left one buffalo for the buzzard people.

How Men First Played the Game of Ball

Apalachee

In ancient times the great chief Ytonaslaq, whose name meant Sleeping Fire in the Apalachee language, had no family but his young granddaughter Nico Taijulo. Her name meant Sun Woman. Sleeping Fire had for an enemy a chief who called himself Lightning Bolt, as if he had great powers. Lightning Bolt lived in a village nearby, and his shamans had told him that one day a son of Sun Woman would kill him. He was full of fear as Sun Woman grew up from childhood.

When Sun Woman was grown, she took up a water jar every morning and went to the stream for water like other daughters and granddaughters. One day, between the village and the stream, she did have a child, a boy. Because she feared that Lightning Bolt would try to kill him if he knew that the child was hers, she hid him in the bushes by the path. She knew that he would soon be found. Then she took up her jar of water and went home to her grandfather, just as she always did.

Panther, Bear, and Jay saw her go. When they came along through the bushes, they found the baby, and argued what to do. "We must take it to

Sleeping Fire," said Jay at last. "He always knows best." And so Bear picked up Sun Woman's son, and they took him to his great-grandfather.

"Do not speak of this child to anyone," Sleeping Fire told Panther, Bear, and Jay. "No one must know that my granddaughter has a son. That one who calls himself Lightning Bolt will be afraid of him, and try to kill him if he hears. We will call the boy Chita."

And so the boy Chita grew up as an orphan, but his great-grandfather and mother made sure that he was cared for. He grew tall and strong, and was better than anyone else at shooting with the bow and arrow. He was better at hitting the rolling stone with his lances in the game of chunkey. He was better at every skill and game. When he was twenty, he was given the strange name of Eslaf-yoopi, though no one but his mother knew what it meant. At the same time his great-grandfather Sleeping Fire warned him again about the man who called himself Lightning Bolt.

Now, the wicked Lightning Bolt had wondered for a long time whether the orphan boy was Sun Woman's son. He thought often of the warning his shamans had given, and when he heard how strong and brave Eslaf-yoopi was, he was afraid. *I must know!* Lightning Bolt thought. Then he thought, *If I can set a trap for Eslaf-yoopi and kill him, at least I will know that he is not the one I should fear.*

So, Lightning Bolt went out looking for the young man, and found him.

"*Hoh,* Eslaf-yoopi!" Lightning Bolt said. "Can you help me? I am making arrowheads and need more flints. It will be a good thing if you bring me a basketful from the bottom of the spring in the Great Sinkhole. They are the best flints."

Eslaf-yoopi agreed, but remembered Sleeping Fire's warning, and went to tell his great-grandfather of all this.

"It is good you come to me," Sleeping Fire said. "The spring in that place is so deep that you might never come up again." He took a handful of shell beads from a pouch and put them in the basket his great-grandson carried. "Hear me: When you come to the Great Sinkhole you will see a little bird diving into the water. Give him these beads, and ask him to bring up flints for you."

Eslaf-yoopi did this, and Diving Bird was happy to have the beads. He brought up flints enough from the bottom of the spring to fill the young man's basket, and Eslaf-yoopi took them to Lightning Bolt. Lightning Bolt was not pleased to see him, but he smiled and thanked him.

"These will do well," he said, "but when I have made the arrowheads, I will need many shafts for my arrows. Can you help me? The best arrows are made from canes that come from the canebrake in the Great

Thicket. It will be a good thing if you cut an arm-
load of canes and bring them to me for my arrows."

Once again Eslaf-yoopi agreed, but again he went
to tell his great-grandfather of all this.

"It is good you come to me," said Sleeping Fire,
"for the canebrake Lightning Bolt spoke of is deep
in the Great Thicket. It is a dangerous place where
there are many poisonous snakes. Hear me: To be
safe, you must make hoops from grapevines and take
them with you. When a snake comes, you must roll
a hoop past it. When each snake turns to chase the
hoop, you can cut canes until the next appears."

Eslaf-yoopi did this, and cut canes until he had
rolled away all of his grapevine hoops. Then he ran
from the canebrake and out of the Great Thicket to
the place where Lightning Bolt was. When Lightning
Bolt saw him he was not pleased, but he smiled and
thanked him.

"These will do well," Lightning Bolt said, "but
when I have fastened the points to all these shafts, I
will need feathers with which to fletch them. Can you
help me? Eagle feathers are best, and there is a nest
of eagles in the tallest tree on the High Hill. It will
be a good thing if you kill the parent eagles for their
feathers, and bring the little eaglets to me alive."

"I will," said Eslaf-yoopi, but this time, too, he
went first to tell his great-grandfather what Lightning Bolt had asked of him.

"Hoh!" said Sleeping Fire. "It is good that you have come to me, for the eagles in the tallest tree kill everyone who tries to rob their nest. They will claw at your hands and try to peck out your eyes so that you will fall. Hear me: You must cut a large gourd to cover your head and two smaller ones to cover the backs of your hands, and you must carry a lariat to throw over and tie up the eagles when they attack you."

And that is what Eslaf-yoopi did. He cut a hole in the bottom of a large gourd and eyeholes to see through, and put it over his head. He tied pieces of gourd over the backs of his hands, and took up his lariat and a basket. Then he went to find the tallest tree on the High Hill and climb it. When he came to the nest in the top of the tree, he caught the eagles and killed them, and plucked out their pinions and tail feathers. He put feathers and the little eaglets in the basket, and he climbed down and took them to Lightning Bolt.

When Lightning Bolt saw Eslaf-yoopi coming, he was dismayed. "None of my tricks can kill this young man," he said to himself. "I must find a way for my warriors to destroy him." So he smiled and thanked Eslaf-yoopi, and said, "When you return home, tell your chief Sleeping Fire that I have thought of a new ball game that will be a good thing for fifty of his people and fifty of mine to play. We will play it with a hard ball on a field with a goal-post. To score a goal, the players must kick the ball so that it hits the post. The first side to make six goals will win, for after eleven goals the game will end."

Eslaf-yoopi thought this ball game a fine idea, and returned to his own village to tell his great-grandfather the news.

"Indeed," said Sleeping Fire, "a new game is a good thing, but this Lightning Bolt has a wicked heart. We must take great care to make good medicine. The players must keep vigil the night before the match, and our old men must search their dreams for omens so that we can place the benches for our players on the lucky side of the field. We will make new fire, too, for a torchbearer to carry at the head of the players on their way to the ball plaza." Old Sleeping Fire smiled. "And when we come there, we will test this one who calls himself Lightning Bolt. We will say that we have only forty-five ballplayers who wish to play."

And all that is what they did. On the day set for the game, Sleeping Fire's people set out with drums and dancing. When they came to the ball game place, Eslaf-yoopi wrapped his feather cloak around him and leaned against a post as if he were feeling ill. When the other side learned that Sleeping Fire was five players short, they would not cut their own side, but hid their glee and said, "Hurry and choose

any five from these watching. We are ready to begin."
Sleeping Fire chose Eslaf-yoopi and four others who
had pretended to be sick or clumsy, and in this way
they tricked the other side into thinking they would
win easily.

The hundred players poured into the middle of
the field, and Lightning Bolt threw the ball among
them. Then the battle began. The players could
only make goals by kicking the ball, but they could
catch it with their hands and run with it until they
were tackled. At once all of the hundred players fell in
a great heap on top of the ball carrier, kicking and
pulling and hitting. The players on the other side
attacked Eslaf-yoopi more than anyone, trying to
break his bones or kill him, but they could not. Eslaf-
yoopi hid his anger until his team had made six
goals, and won, and then—seven! At once he let out a
great roar and a flash that terrified the players and
watchers. It shook the plaza ground under their feet.

"Lightning-Flash! That is what 'Eslaf-yoopi'
means! Eslaf-yoopi is the true Lightning!" the people
cried. "Only the Sun's son could have such power."

"No!" cried the false Lightning Bolt. "I will show
you! I will beat him! I challenge Eslaf-yoopi to a
game of chunkey."

So they played chunkey, but once again the true
Lightning's side won. The false Lightning Bolt feared
for his life, and when the game was over he and his

men ran away. He made fog and mist rise up to hide the way they went, but the true Lightning and the warriors of his great-grandfather Sleeping Fire found and fought and destroyed them.

When Sleeping Fire's people returned to the ball-game ground, they made a special new goal pole in honor of the true Lightning, and ever afterward played the new game of ball in his honor.

THE ICE MAN

Cherokee

Once, long ago, some of the people thought it a good idea to burn a part of the woods in the fall of the year to make a sunny clearing where they could grow corn. The brush burned away and trees were left bare of leaves and branches, but as the fire died down to ashes and smoke, one poplar tree still blazed. It burned and burned until the trunk had burned down to the roots. Then the roots burned on down into the ground until all that was left of the tree was a great hole. When the fire still did not go out but kept on burning a bigger and bigger hole in the earth, the people grew frightened. Water would not put it out. Sand could not put it out. Nothing the people tried could put it out. They began to fear it would grow and grow until it burned up the whole world. "What should we do? What shall we do? What can we do?" they cried.

No one knew. But after a while one old man spoke up. "I have heard of a great man who has power over fire, but he lives far, far to the north, in a house made of ice."

"Then we must send to this Ice Man for help," all the people said.

And so they chose their two finest runners to be messengers. They dressed them in winter furs and gave them parched corn enough for a long journey, and sent them off toward the north. The messengers traveled fast, but they were afraid. The ice country was far away, and in their own country the fire hole burned larger and larger every day. At last they came to the land of snow and ice, and found the Ice Man sitting in the doorway of his icehouse. He was very small, and his white hair hung down to the ground in two braids as long as he was tall.

"Welcome, friends," the Ice Man said to the messengers. He listened to their tale of the great fire hole, and then nodded. "Of course, I will help you." As soon as he said so, he began to unbraid his hair, first one braid and then the other. When it was all loosened, he gathered it up with one hand and struck the hair across the palm of his other hand.

The two messengers felt a cold wind chill their cheeks.

The Ice Man struck his hair across his palm a second time.

The two messengers saw a shower of rain sweep past the door of the icehouse.

The Ice Man struck his hair across his palm for a third time.

The messengers looked out and saw sleet coming down with the rain. When the Ice Man struck

his open palm a fourth time, large hailstones peppered the ground as if he had shaken them from the ends of his hair.

"I am ready now," the Ice Man told them. "You must hurry home. I will follow not far behind you."

So the messengers returned home, and found their people still gathered around the giant fire hole in fear. The next morning a cold wind blew down from the north, and the people were both afraid and glad, for they knew it came from the Ice Man. The wind only made the fire blaze higher. When rain began to fall, the raindrops only seemed to make the fire sizzle more loudly. The rain grew heavy, and sleet and hail poured down with it, and great clouds of smoke and steam boiled up out of the fire hole. The people ran to their houses and covered their doors and windows against the storm. They listened in the dark to the whirlwind as it whipped rain and pounded hailstones into the fire pit.

When at last the flames and smoke were smothered and the storm was gone, the people went out and found a lake where the great fire pit had been. It is still there. If you stand on the shore and listen, sometimes even now you can hear a sound like the crackling of embers in a sleeping fire.

LODGE BOY, WILD BOY, AND THE MONSTER WOMAN

Creek

A hunter, who had been in the forest for many days, shot a deer at last and turned toward home with his prize. His lodge stood apart from the village, close to the woods, and when he came near he called out, "Wife, is the cookfire ready? Tonight we will eat well!"

But his wife did not answer. He looked for her, but found only spilled baskets of corn and nuts and dried berries—and a newborn baby boy.

The man took up the baby and went to the nearest house, but no one was there. The next lodge was empty, too. He called, and soon the people came out of the forest. "We were hiding from the monster Kolowa," they said. "The monster ate up your wife, and we were afraid."

The man's heart was as heavy as stone, for his wife was dear to him. Time passed, and the new son she left behind learned to walk and to talk and to play. Every day he grew dearer to his father. "Stay close to the lodge, and hide if a stranger comes," the father said to the boy each day when he went off to the forest to hunt. He said this because he feared that the monster Kolowa would come back.

One day the father returned to see another small boy playing with his son. The father watched for a while from behind a bush and saw that the boy looked exactly like his own, except that he was naked and his hair was dusty and tangled. When the hunter moved nearer, the strange boy leaped up and ran away as fast as a rabbit or fox.

The next day was the same. The wild boy came to play with Lodge Boy, but when the hunter returned, Wild Boy ran off into the forest. The hunter's heart leaped up. The two boys were so alike that he was sure that they were twins. He was sure that after their mother was killed Wild Boy had been stolen and raised by wild forest animals. He decided to catch the boy the next time he came, and tame him.

The first day the hunter tried, Wild Boy was too fast for him. The second day the hunter took hold of him, but Wild Boy slipped free. On the third day the hunter caught him and set out to tame him with kindness. Wild Boy learned to call him "Father," but he grew only half tame. He still liked best to have his own way.

When Lodge Boy and Wild Boy grew old enough, their father taught them to paddle a canoe. Then, not for the first time, he warned them about the monster Kolowa. "If ever the canoe is on your side of the river, and someone on the far side calls for you to come and paddle them across, first be sure that it is I and no other. Go for no one else. It may be a trick of wicked Old Woman Kolowa, who killed your mother."

"We hear you, Father," said Lodge Boy.

The next day, after the hunter went into the woods to hunt, the boys went to play by the river. Soon they heard a voice cry, "Canoe! Canoe!" and they saw an old woman on the far side.

"Come, young warriors!" she cried. "Come paddle me over to your side."

At once, Wild Boy ran to the canoe and took up a paddle. "Come," he called.

"No!" cried Lodge Boy. "Father said we must not go."

Wild Boy was angry. "You will come," he shouted, "or I will go away and never come back."

So Lodge Boy went with him.

When their canoe reached the far bank, the old woman did not move. "It is hard for me to walk," she said. "People always carry me down to the canoe on their backs. I am not heavy, but you are very young. Perhaps you are not strong enough."

"I *am* strong enough," Wild Boy said loudly, and he sprang from the canoe. Taking the old woman up on his back, he carried her down to the river.

"People always keep me on their backs in the canoe," she said. "I am not heavy, but you are very young. Perhaps you cannot carry me and paddle, too."

"I can!" Wild Boy said proudly, and he stepped into the canoe. With the old woman on his back he could not paddle as well as his brother, but still they reached their own side of the river safely.

Lodge Boy jumped out and pulled the canoe partway up the bank so that the old woman would not have to step in the water

"People always take me on their backs to the top of the bank," the old woman said. "But you are very young. Perhaps—"

"I am strong," said Wild Boy, and he carried her to the top of the bank. Then, before he could put her down, she gave a loud laugh, shouted, *"Kolowai', Kolowai'!"* and stuck fast to his back.

"Get off!" Wild Boy shouted angrily. He hit at her over his shoulder, and his hand stuck. "Get off!" He hit with his other hand, and that stuck, too. "Get off!" He hit back at her with his head, and that stuck to her. He hopped on one foot and kicked back at her with the other and even that stuck, and he fell over.

"Get off!" cried Lodge Boy, and he picked up a thick stick to hit at the old woman. That stuck, too, so he found another and struck her again, but it fastened itself to her like the other. "Old witch, let go my brother," he screamed, and beat at her back with both hands—and he was caught, too. Old Kolowa opened her mouth wide to begin eating them, but the boys shouted and wriggled and rolled her around so that she could not bite one bite.

While they rolled and wriggled and shouted, the boys' father appeared on the far bank of the river. "Canoe! Canoe!" he called, but no one answered. He shaded his eyes to peer over the river, frowned at what he saw, and leaped into the river to swim across. When he reached the other side, he stood with his hands on his hips and looked down at the hungry old-woman monster and the two boys.

"I told you so," he said. "I hope you have learned to listen." And then he walked away to the lodge, built a cookfire, and cooked his dinner. While he ate, he put a large pot of water on the fire. When it boiled, he carried it to the riverbank and poured it over the old woman.

"Ai-ee!" cried the boys as the hot water melted them off the monster.

The old woman shrieked and flew off, crying, *"Kolowai'! Kolowai'!"*

And the hunter went back to finish his dinner.

KEEPER OF THE ANIMALS

Cherokee

That same hunter—the Cherokee call him Kanati—was the best of hunters. From time to time all other hunters came home empty-handed from their hunting, but not Kanati. Every time he took up his bow and went into the forest, he returned with a good, fat buck, or a doe, or a pair of turkeys slung over his shoulder. His sons never went hungry.

Wild Boy thought about this. One day he said to his brother, "Our father must know the best place in all the mountains to find good game. It would be good if we knew where this place might be, and how he kills the game. The next time he goes into the forest, let us follow him and learn these things." Several days later, when they had no meat left, Kanati took up his bow and a few feathers and set out early in the morning to hunt. His sons waited until he was almost out of sight, and then followed.

Not far into the forest, the two boys saw the trees open out ahead. Soon they felt the ground grow soft and wet beneath their feet. They hid behind tree trunks to watch as their father waded out into a swamp where tall *watike* reeds grew. The reeds rattled as a little breeze stirred them.

"How can we follow?" whispered Lodge Boy. "The reeds will tell him we are coming."

"Stay here," said Wild Boy, and he changed himself into a little puff of bird's down and floated up and away. Just as Kanati moved in among the reeds, the little puff of bird's down came to rest on his shoulder. He did not feel or see it, for his eyes were on the reeds. One by one, he chose two of the straightest, and cut them. Then he trimmed both to the same length and gave them points at one end. The feathers he cut and fitted to the other end.

"What can these feathered sticks be for?" Wild Boy wondered. He did not know that hunters used the *watike* reeds to make arrows, because he had never seen an arrow. Kanati did not make arrows at home.

As soon as he finished making the arrows, Kanati made his way out of the swamp and went on. A puff of wind blew the little scrap of bird's down from his shoulder, but he never saw it. When it touched the ground, Wild Boy stood up in his own shape. Swiftly he ran to find his brother and tell him of the strange sticks their father had made in the swamp.

Lodge Boy was as puzzled as Wild Boy. "They must be some magic," he said.

Together, the two brothers hurried after Kanati. They followed him for miles, and always they took care to keep out of sight. Kanati's path took them far up into the mountains until, at last, he stopped by a large rock in a hillside. From their hiding place the brothers watched him lift the rock and move it away from a big, dark hole. At once a large buck came running out of the hole and away. Swiftly, Kanati lifted his bow and shot it with his two arrows. Then he turned and put the large rock back in its place.

"*Hoh!*" said the two boys to each other. "So that is what the sticks he made in the swamp are for!"

"And he keeps a herd of deer holed up in the hill," Lodge Boy whispered.

"Yes!" Wild Boy said. "When we need meat, he comes here, sets one free, and shoots it with the swamp sticks!"

"Come," Lodge Boy urged. "We must hurry home and be there before our father." And so together they ran down the mountain and home. The journey took their father much longer, for he had the heavy deer to carry. He never knew that they had followed him.

Hoh! thought Wild Boy to himself. *I will go back to the mountain and be a great hunter, too!* And he began to look for feathers for the arrows he would make.

One day soon afterward, while the two brothers and their father still had plenty of meat, Wild Boy waited until their father went into the village. Then he told Lodge Boy his plan. Together they took up their father's good bow and second bow and ran off through the forest to the swamp. In the swamp they stopped to cut *watike* reeds and make arrows. When they had a handful of arrows apiece, they left the swamp and ran on into the mountains.

When they came to the hill where the animals were hidden, the brothers between them lifted the big rock to one side. At once a strong, young deer ran out, and before they could raise their bows another ran after him. Then came a doe, and another and another and another. The boys were so startled that they shot without aiming. Because they did not have their father's stong arms, they could draw the bowstrings only a little way, and the arrows did not travel far. As one buck ran past, Wild Boy's shot struck it in the tail. Now, in those days the tails of all deer hung downward, so Wild Boy laughed to see the drooping tail stick straight out behind its owner. Lodge Boy laughed, too, and shot at the next tail to pass by. The deer's tail flipped straight up, so that its furry white underside made a bouncing white marker as the deer bounded away into the forest shadows.

"Again! Again!" shouted Wild Boy happily, and he shot the next deer in the tail so hard that its tail curled up over its back. Both boys liked the look of it that way so much that they used every last arrow to make all the rest of the deer tails curl up and over the same way—and their tails have been like that ever since.

The brothers were enjoying themselves so much that the last deer sprang out and away before they knew it. Before they could put back the great stone, raccoons ran out, too, great numbers of them, and rabbits and squirrels and all kinds of four-footed creatures. After them flocks of turkeys swarmed out, and quail and herons, cranes and pigeons. They rose into the sky in great clouds that darkened the sun, and their wings beat the air with a great noise. At the boys' home far below, the hunter Kanati heard a noise like a great thunderstorm far off in the mountains, and shook his head.

"*Hoh!* So that is where they are! I must go see what trouble those bad boys have stirred up now."

And so he went. When he came to the place in the mountains where he had hidden the game, he saw the boys, the rock, and the opening in the hill. He did not see one bird or animal. His anger was great, but he did not speak a word. Instead, he strode past his sons and into the hill. When he came to the back of the cave, he kicked the lids off the four storage jars that sat there. Out of them swarmed all of the fleas, lice, bedbugs, and gnats that he had kept safely out of the world. In thick clouds, they streamed out of the cave mouth and all over the two brothers.

"*Ee-ee! Ee-ee! Ee-ee!*" screeched Wild Boy.

"*Hah! H-hah! Ha-aah!*" shouted Lodge Boy.

They tried to brush away the insects and could not. The angry insects covered them and bit and stung them. The boys ran. They dropped down and rolled on the ground. Nothing helped. At last they panted and sobbed and lay still. Kanati decided they had been punished enough, and he waved the insects away.

"Hear me, my sons," he said sternly. "You two have always had all the meat you needed, for it was easy for me to come here for a deer or rabbits or turkey. Now hunting will be hard. You will have to search through the whole forest to find even one deer. Sometimes you will go hungry. You will have hard work to keep the insects away. So, go home and think about what you have done." He sighed. "And I will try to find meat for our next meal."

THE THREE OWLS

Tunica

Long ago, four young orphan boys lived together. The oldest was almost as tall as a man, and the youngest came no higher than his middle. They had a house to shield them from the weather, and they never went hungry. They ate venison and turkey, raccoon and possum, pigeon and rabbit and squirrel, for Oldest Brother was a fine shot with his bow and arrow. Every day he went out into the forest to hunt. Every day he took his younger brothers with him.

One day when Oldest Brother took his brothers into the forest to hunt, he sent them on ahead to make camp in their usual place. "If I shoot something, we will eat well. It will be a good thing if you gather wood and make a fire ready to cook it." The three younger brothers watched him go off alone, and then made their way to the camping place.

At the camping place, they gathered wood, cleared the ground, and built and kindled the fire. The shadows of the trees grew long. Night fell. Still, they kept watch for Oldest Brother, but he did not come. At last they wrapped their cloaks around them, lay down, and went to sleep.

In the morning, Older Brother still had not returned. Second Brother thought for a while and then said to the younger two, "It will be a good thing if you feed the fire and guard it. I will go into the forest to look for our brother's tracks and follow them."

The two younger brothers watched Second Brother until he passed out of sight among the trees. During the day they gathered more firewood nearby. Then they sat down to wait for their brothers to return, but dusk fell, and then night, and Second Brother did not come back. They sat up by the fire until the moon rose, and then wrapped their cloaks around them and lay down side by side to sleep.

The next morning came, and still Second Brother had not returned. At midday Third Brother spoke up. "Littlest Brother, I must go into the forest to find our older brothers. It will be a good thing if you stay here to guard the fire and feed it." And he walked off into the forest.

Littlest Brother watched him go, then watched all day for all three to return. Night came, but they did not. Littlest Brother was frightened, but he built the fire up, wrapped his cloak around him, and lay down. His eyes grew heavy, but he could not sleep. He watched the fire, and cried.

Suddenly, a flame from the fire sprang up, gave a twist and a leap, and turned itself into an old man.

"I see you, Littlest Brother," the old fire man said. Then he bent to put a small clay pot on the fire. Soon the liquid in the pot began to boil. After a little while the old man took up the pot in his two hands and squatted down beside the little boy. Next, he took a sip from it and bent over Littlest Brother as if he was going to spit it in his face. Littlest Brother tried to cover his face from the spray, but too late.

"Now you will be strong," the old man said. "Tell me, little one, do you see the pecan tree there, at the edge of the firelight?"

Littlest Brother nodded.

"Tomorrow, little one, you must rise early, go stand by that pecan tree, and give a loud whoop. Then you must jump as high as you can and take hold of the branch that meets your hand. That branch will break off, and from it you will make a bow. Then you must cut and feather arrows. When all this is done, it will be a good thing if you go into the forest to find your brothers."

And that is what Littlest Brother did. He rose before the sun rose. He stood under the pecan tree and whooped and jumped, and pulled down a branch that made a good bow. He cut and pointed and feathered a handful of arrows as well as he could. And then he walked bravely into the woods.

He had not walked far when suddenly he heard

the snap of a twig, and looked up. Straight in front of him stood a deer. Littlest Brother set an arrow to his bow and shot, and the deer fell dead where it stood. Littlest Brother took out his knife and went toward it to skin it, but then he heard another twig snap. He looked around and saw, running toward him with a basket on her arm, the terrible Clawed Witch. She looked like an old woman, but she ran faster than any old woman could. Littlest Brother knew who she was when he saw her long, sharp claws, and the hatchet in her basket.

"Hurry, hurry!" the witch cried as she came near. "Skin the deer, for I'm hungry, hungry!"

Littlest Brother was afraid, for as he moved around the deer to skin it, the witch crept up on him. Around he went, and around again, with the witch coming after. Nearer and nearer she came, and as she came, she took the hatchet out of her basket. Now, Littlest Brother was as brave as he was afraid. He ran at her and snatched her hatchet, and killed her as dead as the deer.

Littlest Brother was still afraid. What if the witch had caught all his brothers with her terrible claws? "Oldest Brother!" he called. "Oh, brothers, where are you?"

There was no answer, and so Littlest Brother set out to follow the witch's tracks back the way she had come. After a while he saw smoke among the trees ahead, and then he saw a house. When he came near it, he saw a cookfire, and two girls sitting near it. When the girls saw him coming, they jumped up and ran into the house.

"Do not be afraid," called Littlest Brother. "I am looking for my three brothers. Have you seen them?"

"Perhaps," said the older girl. "Our grandmother brought three boys. They are in the big soup pot there on the fire."

Littlest Brother went to look into the big soup pot that sat in the hot coals at the side of the cookfire. When he saw the bones simmering in the soup he knew that they belonged to his brothers. At once he scooped out the bones and laid them all out on the ground in order, from the toe bones to the head bones.

"Brothers, I am here," he sang to the bones. "Oh, Brothers, hear me!"

And they did, for the bones sat up and looked at him.

"Brothers, come back, come back!" sang Littlest Brother.

And they did. As soon as he sang, they stood up and were themselves again, in their own skins.

"Do not speak," Littlest Brother warned. "You must follow me home and not look aside. If you look at my heels, but nowhere else, it will be a good thing."

At once, Littlest Brother set out through the forest, and Oldest Brother, Second Brother, and Third Brother followed behind. No one spoke a word, but when a crow cawed in the trees, Third Brother looked aside. Before he could blink he turned into a hoot owl, and flew up to perch in the branches above.

"Oh, Brother!" cried Littlest Brother. "Why did you look aside, dear brother? Now we must leave you behind."

Once again he warned Oldest Brother and Second Brother to watch his heels as they walked, and not look aside. Then he set off again for home. No one spoke a word, but when a squirrel chattered in a tree, Second Brother looked aside. Before he could blink he turned into a horned owl and flew up to perch in the branches above.

"Oh, Brother!" cried Littlest Brother. "Twice I warned you not to look aside! Now only Oldest Brother is left to me, and we must leave you behind." And he warned Oldest Brother yet again to watch his heels and not to look aside as they made their way home.

As they walked, neither boy spoke a word, but when a deer snorted off among the trees, Oldest Brother looked aside. Before he could blink, he turned into a screech owl and flew up to perch in the branches above.

Littlest Brother cried out, "Oh, Brother! Why did you look aside? Now I am all by myself, and I must leave you behind."

And he wept many tears as he went home alone.

THE WONDERFUL
SKY BOAT

Alabama

On a day long ago, in the Old Time, a great canoe full of people came sailing down from the sky. They laughed and sang as they came, and when the canoe touched down on the earth they sprang out and began to play a game of ball. When the game was finished, they climbed back into the canoe and began to sing as they had before. As the song rose, the boat rose, and they soared up into the sky. Their singing and laughter floated down to earth as they flew out of sight.

The next day the great canoe came sailing down again. Just as before, the people who sailed in it laughed and sang as they came. The wonderful canoe landed in the same grassy place, and the people leaped out and began a game of ball, just as before. When the game was over, they returned to the sky boat. Singing their songs, they soared up into the sky and vanished.

Every day they came for their game.

But one day a hunter was tracking a deer through the trees nearby as they came. He heard the singing and the laughter, and wondered who it could be, for no people lived nearby. As he drew near the open place, he climbed onto the trunk of a fallen tree to see over the tops of the bushes. He still heard singing, but saw no one. Then the wonderful sky boat sailed down and came to rest at the edge of the grassy place.

The man watched from his hiding place as the ball game began. Suddenly, one of the players threw the ball toward him, and it rolled into the bushes. A young woman came running after it. Her eyes sparkled, and she laughed as she ran, and as she came near the hunter ran out and caught hold of her. The ball players took fright and ran to the great canoe. The young woman cried out, but the others climbed in, breathlessly singing, and swooped up and away toward the far-off sky dome.

The young woman was so beautiful that the hunter had loved her at once, and so he took her home and married her. In time they had three children. One day the small children said to their father, "Father, will you go hunting? For too long we have had no fresh meat. Take up your bow and arrows and go hunt the deer."

"I will," said their father. He took up his bow and arrows and set out, but when he had gone only a little way from home his heart grew heavy within him. Already he missed his dear wife and children. He stopped to look around him, and when he saw no deer, he turned and went home.

His wife saw him coming, and said to their children, "Go say to your father, 'Oh, Father, we are hungry for meat. Go farther off and find us a deer. We need venison to make us grow strong.'" So the children ran to him and said, "Oh, Father, we are hungry for meat. Go farther off and find us a deer. We need venison to make us grow strong."

"Then I will," said their father, and he went.

As soon as he was gone, his wife and children ran to his canoe where it lay on the riverbank and climbed in. They began to sing, and as they sang the canoe lifted into the air. The hunter, though, had gone only a little way. When he heard the song he ran back at once. "Oh, do not leave me!" he cried, and he leaped up to catch hold of the canoe as it rose. When he had pulled it to the ground, his wife and children stepped out and went about their work and play as if nothing had happened. For a while after that he watched them carefully, but his wife made a small canoe in secret, and hid it under the bushes.

After a time the man decided it was safe to go hunting again. As soon as he was gone, the woman brought out the small canoe and put the children into it. Then she jumped into the larger one and cried out, "Sing! Sing!"

She sang, and the children sang, and the canoes rose into the air, but once again her husband had heard their singing. He ran home in great fear and

saw the two canoes float upward. "Oh, do not leave me!" he cried. But he could not leap up after both boats, and so he sprang up to catch the small canoe and bring his children back to earth. Their mother shut her eyes and sang on, and as she sang her canoe flew up through the clouds and vanished.

The children wept. "We want to follow our mother," they cried to their father. "And so do I," said he. So he climbed into the canoe with them and began to sing the song he had heard. The children sang, too. The canoe soared up and up and up, and came at last to the land above the sky. They landed, and walked on until they came to a house where an old woman lived.

To the old woman, the man said, "We have come to see my wife. We have come to see their mother."

The old woman nodded. "She is at the next house along, dancing, always dancing. But you must eat before you go." And she cooked them some little squashes. *Too little, too little,* the children thought, for they were very hungry. But no matter how much they ate, a little was left. When they had eaten all they could and were ready to go, the old woman broke a corncob in pieces and gave each child a piece.

At the next house the people said, "Yes, she is here. She is dancing." And they saw her dancing. She danced and danced, and she looked at them, but she did not see them. The children threw a piece of corncob at her, but missed. They stood before her, and she danced right through them. The next time she danced past they threw another piece of corncob. It missed, too, but she said, "I smell something," as she danced by. When they threw the last bit of corncob, it hit her and her eyes opened wide. "My children have come!" she cried.

So they went all together to the two canoes and returned together to this world. But the next time the man went hunting, his wife and children got into his canoe, and sang and laughed themselves up to the land beyond the sky.

When the man returned home, he tried for a while to live alone, but he could not. So he stepped into the small canoe and began to sing. As he sang, the canoe sailed up into the sky, but when he looked down at the country he had left behind, his heart grew so heavy that he forgot to sing. He forgot to sing, and he could not laugh. And his sky boat fell back to earth.

THE OLD PEOPLE WHO TURNED INTO BEARS

Chitimacha

In the village between the river and the edge of the forest, two baby boys who were orphans lived with an old man and his old wife. People thought the old man and old woman were the boys' uncle and aunt, but they were so old that when the boys learned to talk, they called them Grandmother and Grandfather.

Grandmother cared for and cooked for and sang to them. When they were old enough to understand, she showed them how to plant corn and tan skins into leather, and sew moccasins for themselves. Grandfather hunted each day for the meat they ate, and when they were old enough to learn, he taught them how to make bows and feather arrows, and to know the tracks of every animal.

And so it went until the boys were half grown. Then one day the old woman said, as she said every day, "The woodpile grows low, and I must go to the forest to gather more. I shall be back before you have shelled the corn for grinding." And she went.

The morning went by, and Grandmother did not return. When the sun stood overhead, the corn was shelled and the boys began to be frightened.

"Grandmother knows her way in the woods. Do not fear for her," the older of the two said bravely. But as the afternoon shadows grew longer, he said, "Let us go into the forest to find her."

Together they set out on the path into the forest to look for Grandmother. They did not go far before they heard a rustling in the bushes. When they turned, they saw a she-bear watching them.

"Grandmother!" the younger boy called, and he ran toward the bear.

"No, Brother! That is not Grandmother. Let her be!" cried the older. He sprang after his little brother, to stop him and pull him back to the path. But he saw how the she-bear's black eyes followed them.

Together, the boys ran all the way home. There they found Grandfather had returned from his hunting with two pheasants.

"Grandfather, Grandfather!" Little Brother cried. "We went into the forest to find Grandmother, and she has hair all over."

"Grandmother went to gather wood," Older Brother said. "And we saw a bear."

"Hoh!" said Grandfather, and he nodded. "All will be well. I will go to gather wood. While I am gone, you must grind the corn into meal, and pluck the birds for roasting."

So Older Brother ground the corn, and Little Brother scooped the meal into a bowl. Little Brother plucked the feathers from the birds, and Older Brother cleaned them ready for roasting. The sun slipped down behind the treetops, but still Grandfather did not return.

Little Brother cried as he mixed meal and water into cakes. Older Brother tried not to cry as he built and lit the cookfire. They cooked and ate the cakes and meat. The last wood from the woodpile was burned to ash. Then they went indoors and lay down on their sleeping mat, and Older Brother sang Little Brother to sleep.

The next morning, because they had no wood for the morning cookfire, the brothers set out to gather wood. They did not go far along the forest path before they heard a noise in the bushes behind them. Turning, they saw the dark shape of a bear run away.

They found a few sticks of wood, and carried them home to make a small cookfire. Soon Grandmother came, with more wood for the fire, and baked corn cakes. Grandfather came at midday with two fine rabbits.

The brothers were happy until Grandmother said, "There is no wood now for the evening cookfire. Grandfather and I will go for more. We will be back before you have swept the floor mats and filled the water pots from the river."

When they did not return, the children went again to look for them. Once again, they saw a bear, but the bear ran away. Little Brother and Older Brother cried, but soon Older Brother dried his tears. He sang a song to cheer away Little Brother's fears, and they went home again, gathering wood on the way.

For three days Grandmother and Grandfather went away and came back. Each time they found Little Brother and Older Brother safe and well, and well-fed.

The fourth day, the old people went and never returned.

But there were always two bears nearby in the forest.

PANTHER
AND LITTLE SISTER

Creek

Long ago, four brothers lived with their beautiful little sister in a house on the bank of a river. Their mother and father were dead, but the older brothers looked after the younger one and their sister, who was the youngest of all.

One day, the panther named Istepahpah, which means "Man-eater," overheard one of the Creek people tell another about the beautiful little girl who lived in the house on the riverbank. "Her black hair is as shiny as a raven's wing," the woman said. "Her black eyes sparkle like stars. When she laughs, her teeth are as bright as river pearls."

"I must see this child," the Panther Istepahpah said to himself. So the next morning he stepped into his dugout canoe, paddled down the stream, and waited until he saw her brothers go off into the forest to hunt. Then he paddled down to the house and called out to the little girl, who sat in the doorway shelling beans.

"Hoh, little girl, come step into my boat," Panther called in a kind, grandfatherly voice.

"Oh, no, I must never go with strangers," Little Sister answered. Her brothers had warned her about such dangers.

"Of course you must not," said Panther, kindly. "I did not mean that I would take you out on the river." He stepped out and pulled the canoe a little way up onto the bank. "I wanted to show you the three little panthers I have in the basket in my canoe. They are small and soft and new. Come, see!"

Now, Little Sister wanted very much to see the three little panthers, and so she went down the river-bank to the water's edge to look. "There is a lid on the basket," she said.

"To keep them from falling out and into the water," explained Panther. He smiled. "Do not be afraid. I would never eat a pretty little girl. I will sit down here on the bank, out of the way. You can climb in and look for yourself." And he sat down on the bank a little way apart from the canoe.

So Little Sister climbed into the canoe and lifted the lid off Panther's basket, but even before she could see that it was empty, the Panther Istepahpah had sprung from the bank into the canoe and pushed it away from the shore. "No!" cried Little Sister, but then she was silent, for there was no one to hear her cries.

"Do not be frightened," Panther said in his silky voice as he paddled upstream. "I am taking you home with me. I need a little girl to help my wife, and you will do very well."

When they reached Panther's home, Istepahpah called his wife and said, "I have brought a little girl to help you." Early the next morning before he went off to the forest to hunt, he said to Little Sister, "Take some acorns from the storage basket and wash them in the river. I love acorn soup! Have them soaked and ready when I bring home the meat to cook with them in the soup."

After he was gone, Panther's wife sighed. "I am sad that he has brought you here, little girl. He is cruel to me, and he is sure to be cruel to you, too. We must hope that he brings home meat from his hunt. When he does not, he puts a little bit of me into his acorn soup, and he will do the same to you. I cannot bear to think of that. I must find a way to help you to escape. Where will you go?"

"Home to my brothers' house," said Little Sister.

Panther's wife thought for a moment, and went to fetch the acorns. Then she called out, "Koti! Koti!" and Koti the water frog hopped up from the stream. "Will you wash and soak the acorns for this little girl to help her escape from Panther?" Panther's wife asked him.

"I will," answered Koti.

"That is good," she said. "And will you answer 'No' when Istepahpah comes home and calls out, 'Are my acorns washed and soaked?'"

"I will," said Koti. He took the gourd bowl full of acorns from her, and hopped with it back down to the river.

Then Panther's wife said to Little Sister, "Istepah-pah has magic that can smell out footsteps, so you must not leave the house by the door and the path. You will have to climb over the roof and slip into the forest behind the house." And she helped her to do just that.

Not long afterward, Panther returned. "Little girl," he growled, "have you washed and soaked my acorns?"

"No," called Koti from the riverside.

After a little while Panther asked again. "Little girl, have you washed and soaked my acorns?"

Koti once again called, "No."

How can she be so slow? Panther wondered, and he went down toward the river. Koti heard him coming, and jumped into the water. Panther came too late to see him, but heard the splash and thought it was the little girl. He slipped into the water to follow her, calling out in his sweetest voice, "Little girl, little girl! Why do you run away from me?" He swam up and down and when he did not find her, climbed out and went to his house. There he took out his Motarkah, a magic wheel that was a finder-of-lost-things.

Panther threw Motarkah along the path by his house. It rolled a little way and rolled back. He threw it along the path in the other direction. It rolled a little way and came back. He tried other directions, but each time it returned to him. At last he gave up and threw it down in front of his house. Off it went, up the wall, over the roof, and into the forest, following Little Sister's trail. Panther followed it at a run, and soon caught a glimpse of Little Sister running far ahead.

Little Sister was running as fast as she could, and she sang to herself as she ran. *"I wonder whether I can come to my brothers' house before he catches me. I wonder whether I will come to my brothers' house before he catches me!"*

At her brothers' house far off beside the river, her youngest brother, Kutche-helochee, was parching some corn over the fire. Suddenly he stopped and ran to find his brothers. "Brothers, I heard my sister singing!" he cried.

"We hear nothing," they answered. "Return to your work, Little Brother."

In the forest, Little Sister raced on, with the magic wheel and Panther coming nearer all the time. Under her breath she sang, *"I wonder, can I come to my brothers' house before he catches me. I wonder, will I come to my brothers' house before he catches me!"*

Far off, Little Brother Kutche-helochee jumped up from the fire and ran to his brothers. "I hear my sister singing. We must go to find her. We must!" His brothers heard nothing, but they agreed to go with Kutche-helochee into the forest, for they knew that Little Brother believed what he said. He did not tell lies. They took up their bows and arrows and followed him.

In the forest, as they ran, they all heard Little Sister's breathless song. *"I wonder . . . wonder. Can I come . . . come to my brothers' house. Before he catches . . . catches me? I wonder . . . wonder. Will I, will I?"*

The three older brothers stopped Kutche-helochee. "Stay here, Little Brother," they said. "You are too young to help us. Stay here, out of danger."

But Kutche-helochee would not stay. He followed, and soon the brothers saw Little Sister running with the magic Motarkah and Panther close behind her. The brothers shot their arrows at Motarkah, but the arrows bounced off it and it rolled on past them. Little Sister ran on until she reached the house. Motarkah rolled after her, but Kutche-helochee turned and ran after the wheel. He struck it with the little wooden paddle he had used to stir the corn as it parched and Motarkah rolled over onto its side, and stopped.

Istepahpah the Panther kept on. He passed the brothers so fast that their arrows missed him, but when he came near the house Kutche-helochee ran up to him and hit him so hard with the little wooden paddle that he killed him.

From that day on, Little Sister and the brothers called Little Brother the bravest warrior of all.

The Country Under the Water

Tunica

Once, long ago, in a village that lay where a river met the sea, strange things happened in the night. Sometimes people woke up and heard hens cackling out across the water even though there were no islands there. Other times, melons that hung on their vines at nightfall were gone in the morning. Some nights they heard a rooster's *cock-a-doodle-oo!* ring out across the waves. Sometimes the noise of dogs barking came to them across the moonlit sea.

One morning on the day after a feast, a man of the village rose early to go hunting, and his wife rose with him to tend her garden. When they opened the door to their house, they found a young woman they had never seen before sitting on the ground outside. Her face was streaked with tears.

"Please," she said. "May I live with you?"

The man and his wife did not know what to say. "Who are you?" they asked. Other people came to stare at her. "Who are you?" they asked, too.

The young woman answered their question with a question. "At nightfall, do you sometimes hear what sounds like a rooster's crow?"

"We do."

"In the night do you sometimes hear what sounds like hens clucking?"

"We do."

"And dogs barking?"

"We do," they said. "But why do you ask?"

"It was not chickens or dogs," she said. "It was my people you heard out on the sea. Sometimes we come to your gardens. Last night my friends came and ate melons, but I smelled a beautiful smell and tasted from a dish left from your feast." She wept more tears. "It tasted as fine as it smelled, but it is forbidden for our people to eat food that is cooked. Because I have done this bad thing, they say I cannot go home. May I stay here with you?"

The man and his wife looked on her kindly. "Yes, you may stay." So she followed them, and lived with them.

Before long, a young man of the village fell in love with her and won her and married her, and took her to his home. They lived together happily, and had three boy children, but when seven years had passed, the young woman grew sad. "The time of my punishment is over," she said. "The time for me to return to my home has come. You must take good care of the boys, for I must go."

Her husband was full of grief, and he begged her to stay. He followed her as she walked to the shore of the sea. "Oh, wife," he cried, "do not leave me. Oh, do not!"

The woman said sadly, "I must. The time has come." And she walked into the sea. When the water was waist-deep, she dived under and was gone. Her husband turned and went home.

For seven long years he took care of his boys and grieved for his lost wife. At the end of the seventh year, his wife came walking out of the sea. "I am come back to you for now," she said. "After seven years I must go away again, but in seven years our sons will be grown. If you wish, I can take you with me."

"And I will go," he said.

When the seven years had passed, they went together to the ocean shore and walked into the water. When the water came up to their waists, the wife told him, "Watch where I dive, for you must dive through the ripple my feet make as I go."

So he did. And as they went under the water they came at last to a door, and that door opened into a wide country, and the people there came to meet them, and the man and his wife never again returned to the world above.

ABOUT THE STORYTELLERS

THE SOUTHEASTERN PEOPLES

In the centuries since the early Spanish explorers met the Timucuas on the Florida coast in the year 1513, most of the Native American tribes that have lived in the Southeast have vanished. Soon after the Europeans appeared, whole villages and even tribes died out, and their stories with them, for the new-comers brought smallpox and other terrible diseases with them from the Old World. In the centuries that followed, more tribes were destroyed in disputes or wars with their neighbors, or with the Spanish, French, or English. Still more tales were lost, though a few were recorded by early Spanish mission priests in Florida. It was not until the late nineteenth century, when most of the peoples were scattered or gone, that outsiders began to take an interest in the tales, and to write them down. In *The Wonderful Sky Boat,* I have retold some of the stories they saved for us. The storytellers were:

THE ALABAMA

In 1702 there were perhaps four hundred families of Alabama in their historic homeland on the upper Alabama River. Their language was Muskhogean, and most closely related to that of the Koasati.

The French, newly established at Mobile, and the Alabama soon became allies, and remained good friends. In 1717 the French set up Fort Toulouse in Alabama country, where the Alabama took in the Tawasa and Pawokti tribes, refugees from Florida. After 1763, when the English took over from the French, some Alabama moved south to join the Seminole in Florida. Others went with the Koasati to the Tombigbee River, then later returned to their home country. Still others went to the Mississippi River Valley, and then west into Louisiana and on to Polk County, Texas, where their descendants still live on the Alabama-Coushatta Reservation. Those who stayed on in Alabama fought in the Creek-American War and lost all their lands as a result. With the Creeks, they trekked to Oklahoma, where their descendants still live.

THE APALACHEE

Their name may mean "people on the other side" or, perhaps, "helper." Their homeland was the area around present-day Tallahassee, Florida. Spanish explorers first met them there in 1528. In 1607, when the Spanish had established missions across northern Florida, the Apalachee invited them to send missionaries into their country. In time, most of the Apalachee were baptized into the Christian religion. They remained at peace with the Spanish, but in the early eighteenth century, a great Apalachee war party invaded Creek country to the north. They were defeated, and not long afterward the English, allies of the Creeks, swept down from South Carolina. They destroyed most of the Apalachee towns and carried off great numbers of people from the others. Many of these captives escaped after a time and returned to Florida. Others traveled. In 1764, England took control of Florida and the French and Spanish lands west to the Mississippi, and the Apalachee moved on to Spanish Louisiana. In 1803, they sold their land there, and of the small numbers who were left, some became wanderers. Some were absorbed into other tribes, and others moved with the Creeks to Oklahoma. A nation of seven thousand or more had vanished like a morning mist.

THE BILOXI

The Biloxi, whose language—unlike any of their neighbors—was Siouian, apparently migrated to Louisiana from the north and east by way of Alabama. During the first half of the eighteenth century they seem to have moved every few years, but settled eventually on the Pearl River in Mississippi. Not long after the French gave up their holdings east of the Mississippi in 1763, the Biloxi moved west to Louisiana and up the Red River. When they sold their lands there early in the nineteenth century, some remained on the river, but a large number migrated to Texas, then back to return to Louisiana or on to Oklahoma. By the middle of the twentieth century the tribe was practically extinct, except for a few living in Louisiana, or in the Choctaw Nation.

THE CADDO

The southeastern Caddo peoples include the Nachitoches Confederacy and the Adai in Louisiana. The name Nachitoches was said to mean "place where the earth is the color of red ochre," and they lived in northwestern Louisiana. In 1702, their crops failed and the Nachitoches traveled down to a French fort on the Mississippi where the commander welcomed them and sent them to live with the Acolapissa tribe on Lake Pontchartrain. In 1713-14 this same commander organized their return to their own country, and set up a post there that he commanded until his death in 1744. The Nachitoches prospered in trading with peoples to the north and west, but dwindled in numbers. In later years, some stayed on in their own country, but in the late eighteenth century they sold a large portion of their land to the French Creoles. Of those who stayed on, most died out or were assimilated. Others left to join their Kadohadacho and Hasinai relatives farther west.

The Adai, a tribe of about four hundred that French explorer Iberville met in 1699 and called the "Natao," lived in the area of present-day western

Nachitoches County. Spanish missionaries established a mission among them in 1717, and a military post soon afterward. Both were abandoned about 1773. By 1805, only one small Adai settlement was known. The survivors are thought to have joined the Hasinai, Kadohadacho, or Eyeish, western Caddoan tribes that later were gathered into a combined Caddo reservation in the Oklahoma Indian Territory.

THE CATAWBA

The Catawba of the Carolinas were first known as the Issa—a word that means "river"—after their home on the Catawba River. The Spanish met them during an expedition northward into South Carolina in 1566, but it was the English who claimed and colonized their homeland. In the early eighteenth century the Catawba became allies of the English against the Tuscarora. Except for their part in the Yamassee uprising several years later, they were loyal friends of the colonists. There were once about five thousand Catawba, but smallpox, liquor, and warfare with other tribes reduced their numbers. Many of their descendants were absorbed into other tribes or the general population. The few who were not live mostly in South Carolina.

THE CHEROKEES

Cherokee may mean "people of a different speech" in the Muskhogean Creek language. The Cherokees spoke a "foreign" tongue distantly related to those of the Iroquoian tribes. Their traditions told that they had come to their old lands in Tennessee and Carolina from somewhere to the northeast. The English first met them when traders from Virginia ventured into the mountains, and the two nations were allies until 1759. In that year, war broke out after the hostile governor of South Carolina took captive some twenty great men of the Cherokee, and his soldiers murdered them. In 1761, at the governor's request, a British army was sent to the colony to invade Cherokee country. It destroyed the Lower Towns and forced the tribe to make peace. Because of their mistrust of the land-hungry colonists, the Cherokee sided with the British in the American Revolution and went on fighting for their lands afterward. In 1820 they formed their own government, but many lost heart and moved west to Arkansas territory.

In the end, the settlers and government forced the Cherokee nation to sell the last of their lands and move in 1838-39 to the Indian Territory in what is now Oklahoma. Except for several hundred who hid in the mountains, they were forced to make the westward journey in midwinter, in great hardship. Almost a quarter of them died on the journey that came to be called "the Trail of Tears." The present-day Western Cherokees still live in

Oklahoma. The Eastern Cherokees of the Carolinas are the descendants of those who fled into the mountains in 1838.

THE CHITIMACHA

The lands of the Chitimacha of the Louisiana Gulf Coast were along Grand River, Grand Lake, and lower Bayou La Teche. Chitimacha may mean "Grand River" in their language. France claimed the Louisiana Territory, and in 1699 the colony of New France enlisted the Chitimacha as allies. That friendship did not last long—for the twelve years from 1706 to 1718, the Chitimacha were at war with the French. When the struggle was over, many of the Chitimacha were made slaves, and their people were forced to settle on a reservation along the Mississippi. By 1881 most of those lands were lost to them, and all that remains is a small reservation in St. Mary Parish, the home of the present-day tribe.

THE CHOCTAW

The meaning of their name is not known, but they were also called "Flat Heads" by the English, French, and some other tribes. The name came from their custom of flattening the foreheads of babies to make their heads a shape they thought more handsome.

The Choctaw were the largest of the southeastern tribes, except for the Cherokee. Most of their hun-

dred or so towns lay in southeastern Mississippi
and in nearby Alabama. The early Spanish explorer
De Soto met them, and later the tribe had good
relations with the French traders who came among
them. When the English acquired all the lands east
of the Mississippi, the Choctaw, under the influence
of their great man Pushmataha, lived in peace with
them, too. Even so, groups began moving across the
Mississippi. In 1830, when the Choctaw were forced
to cede their homelands to the government, many
more moved on to the Indian Territory in Oklahoma. Others stayed behind on reservation lands in
Mississippi, where their descendants still live.

THE CREEKS

The Muskogee of Georgia and Alabama were an
important early group of related tribes whose traditions said that their ancestors came from the
northwest. The early Spanish explorers met them
first, in the mid-sixteenth century. Gradually the
Muskhogean tribes drew a number of the neigh-
boring peoples, such as the Guale, Oconee, and
Apalachee, into a confederacy of tribes. Together
they came to be called "Creeks" because those whom
the earliest English colonists met lived along a river
the Englishmen knew as Ocheese Creek. Later, the
northerly tribes were known as "Upper Creeks,"
and the southerly, "Lower Creeks."

Because the Creek country lay between the Spanish, French, and English colonies, each colony sought their friendship as a protection against the others. For a long time, the Creeks were allies of the English. When the English sought to win Florida from Spain, the Creeks made war against the Floridian tribes and helped to destroy them. After 1763, when Florida became English, some Creek tribes, who would come to be known as Seminoles, moved south into the then-empty lands. In 1813 most of the Upper Creeks made war against the Americans, but many Lower Creeks took the American side. The Upper Creeks lost, and this division deepened in 1825 when pro-American chiefs were persuaded to sign a treaty giving up all Creek lands. Reluctantly, between fifteen thousand and twenty thousand Creeks moved west to Oklahoma between 1836 and 1840. In time the two groups united again and elected their own government, which lasted until Oklahoma became a state.

THE HITCHITI

One of the tribes of the Creek Confederacy, the Hitchiti were counted among the Lower Creeks. They were the largest of the group of tribes who spoke the Hitchiti or Atsik-hata language. When the early Spanish explorers came, the Hitchiti lived on the lower Ocmulgee River in Georgia. They later moved to what is now Chattahoochee County in Georgia and, in the Great Removal of the nineteenth century, were forced by the government to move west to Oklahoma. There, in time, they merged with the other peoples of the Creek Confederacy.

THE KOASATI

The Koasati were members of the Muskhogean family of languages. The meaning of their name, sometimes given as Coosawda or Coushatta, is unknown. Sixteenth-century Spanish explorers may have met them in their old homeland on the Tennessee River, but in the latter seventeenth-century they moved south to the Coosa and upper Alabama Rivers of Alabama, among the Upper Creeks. At the end of the eighteenth century some moved across the Mississippi, and others followed. Some of these bands went as far as east Texas, but most returned to Louisiana. Of those who stayed behind in Alabama, a few joined the Seminoles in Florida, but most went with the Creeks to the Indian Territory in Oklahoma in the Great Removal.

THE NATCHEZ

In the early years, the Natchez—pronounced *Natchay,* with the z silent—were the strongest of the peoples on the lower Mississippi. They spoke a language distantly related to the Muskhogean languages, but they were descendants of an earlier and very different culture. That older culture, the "Mississippian," is also called the Temple Mound Builders. The chief town of the Natchez—also called Natchez—was near the site of the present-day city of that name. There, a number of great mounds—think of them as shaped like pyramids with the top halves cut off—stood near a broad plaza. A temple stood atop the largest, and the tops of the others held the houses of the ruler, the Great Sun, of his mother, his brother Suns, and the Woman Suns, his sisters. In the surrounding town lived the nobles, the "honored men," and the ordinary people, whom the upper classes called Stinkards. The word meant "a mean and nasty person," just as the word "stinker" does today, but in those days "mean and nasty" meant "low-class and dirty," not "unkind and unpleasant," as it does now.

The Natchez were hostile to the Spanish, and to the French when they first came. They later made peace with the French and lived for the most part at peace with them until 1729. In that year a commander of the nearby French fort made enemies of them, and they destroyed the fort and French settlement. The war ended with the surrender of many Natchez and the flight of the rest. Those who escaped divided into two bands, one settling with the Upper Creeks and the other with the Cherokee, and in the next century they moved west with these peoples to Oklahoma.

THE SEMINOLES

The name Seminole is said to mean "one who has camped away from the regular towns," but their own name for themselves has been *Ikaniuksalgi,* or "peninsula people." They were not one people, but made up of groups from a number of tribes. The Oconee and Miccosukee were the first to move south into Florida, in about 1750. Before long they were joined by Muskogee Creeks, along with groups of Hitchiti, Alabama, Yamassee, and Yuchi. Still more Creeks came in 1814 after the Creek-American War. The Seminoles themselves fought two wars with the Americans. The second, inspired by the great Osceola, lasted for seven years, until 1842. Three thousand captured Seminoles were shipped to Oklahoma, and the rest were driven south into the Everglades. One band later took the government's offer of peace and money in exchange for moving west to the Indian Territory. Many, though, stayed in the Everglades, still undefeated.

THE TUNICA

Tunica means "the people," but they called themselves *Yoron.* They, the Chitimacha, Atakapa, Ofo, Koroa, and Yazoo made up the "Tunican language group." It appears that the Spanish explorer De Soto met Tunican tribes west of the Mississippi in the sixteenth century, and the French learned of them in the next century. Their homeland was along the lower Yazoo River, and a number of their villages were known for salt making. In 1706, the Tunica moved to a town of the Houma people, but later attacked the Houma and took their land near the Red River. They were also resented because they became allies of the French in conflicts with the Natchez and other tribes north along the river. Those tribes made war on them in 1731. The remaining Tunica stayed in that region until the end of the century, when they moved up the Red River to Avoyel country. Some stayed in that country, and others later settled among the Atakapa or among the Choctaw in Oklahoma.

THE YAMASSEE

The meaning of the name Yamassee is not known for certain, but their language was Muskhogean, and probably related most closely to the Hitchiti. Their early lands were on the Ocmulgee River in Georgia. The Spanish may have met them as early as 1521. In the 1630s, the Yamassee and their allies made peace with the Apalachee, and invited the Spanish to send missionaries to them. After 1675 there were five Yamassee missions in northern Florida, but ten years later the Yamassee left the Spanish missions for South Carolina. There, the English gave them lands near the mouth of the Savannah River, but in 1715 they rebelled against the English. Defeated, they fled south and remained allies of the Spanish until the Spanish lost Florida to the English. As their numbers dropped, the Yamassee were scattered. Some lived among the Apalachee, some with the Creeks. Some settled once more on the Savannah River and were known as the Yamacraw, but later moved south again. Others were among the bands that in time became the Seminole.

THE YUCHI

The Yuchi spoke a language different from those of their neighbors, and the name Yuchi may come from "Ochesee" or "Ocheese," a name the Hitchiti and others gave to people speaking languages not related to their own. The earliest-known homeland of the Yuchi was in eastern Tennessee, but they had settlements farther east, west, and north as well. Spanish records tell of Yuchi raids into Florida in 1639 and later. One band settled in West Florida until the mid-eighteenth century, when they moved north to join the Upper Creeks. A few moved south in Florida to join the Seminole. The Yuchi on the Savannah River in Georgia joined the Lower Creeks in 1751, and in the next century moved with them to Oklahoma.

Those who remained in Tennessee, in Cherokee country, probably made the forced migration to Oklahoma with the Cherokees in 1838-39.

ABOUT THE STORIES

Most of the tales I have retold in *The Wonderful Sky Boat* were first written down long after the storytellers' tribes had lost their own homelands and moved to Oklahoma or to reservations. Some had clearly been handed down, generation by generation, for hundreds of years. A few are very old indeed. Others are tales told by peoples living with other tribes, and may have taken details from the tales they heard from neighbors. Traditionally, though, Native American storytellers tried to tell a story just as they had heard it from their elders. European travelers or missionaries—and, later, American scholars—wrote down the tales. It was in their published articles or collections of tales that I found them.

For some of the tales I have retold, I was able to choose the version I thought most interesting from among those from three or four different tribes. For most of the stories, my retelling is based on a single storyteller's version, but for several I drew on more than one old telling of a tribe's tale. Like most storytellers retelling tales that do not come from their own tribes or families, I tell them and write them down in my own words (and sometimes give them new titles).

My most important sources for the stories are listed below. Many of the books are found only in very large libraries, but you may find those marked with an asterisk (*) in your public library or in a bookstore:

Douglas Summers Brown, in *The Catawba Indians: The People of the River* (1966), reprints Charles Lanman's retelling of the story of the "First Woman."

An article in the *Bulletin of the Bureau of American Ethnology,* no. 47 (1912), includes "Why the Buzzard Is Bald." *Bulletin* no. 132 (1942) gives a summary of the myth about "The Crying Place." *Bulletin* no. 133 (1942) includes a version of "The Old People Who Turned into Bears." "The Rabbit Who Stole Fire" appears in *Bulletin* no. 161 (1956). *Bulletin* no. 196 (1966) includes a version of the story I have named "Bigfoot Bird."

David I. Bushnell, Jr., in "Myths of the Louisiana Choctaw," in *American Anthropologist,* N.S. no. 12 (1910), recounts the tale I call "How the Biters and Stingers Got Their Poison."

George A. Dorsey, in *Traditions of the Caddo* (1905), recounts the tale of "The Girl Who Married a Star."

Mary R. Haas, in "Tunica Texts" in *University of California Publications in Linguistics,* vol. 6 (1950), prints "The Three Owls" and "The Country Under the Water" in Tunican and English translation.

H. S. Halbert, in an article in *Mississippi Historical Society Publications,* vol. 2 (1899), summarizes a version of "The Coming of Corn."

John H. Hann, author of *Apalachee: The Land Between the Rivers* (1988), reprints in English the version of "How Man Learned the Game of Ball," which the missionary friar Juan de Paiva wrote in Spanish in 1676.

* George E. Lankford, in *Southeastern Legends: Tales from the Natchez, Caddo, Biloxi, Chickasaw, and Other Nations* (1987), reprints versions of "Stonecoat," "Lodge-Boy, Wild Boy, and the Monster Woman," and "Keeper of the Animals."

* James Mooney's *Myths of the Cherokee* (1970) is reprinted from the *19th Annual Report of the U.S. Bureau of American Ethnology* (1900), and it includes "How Rabbit Stole Otter's Coat," and "The Ice Man."

John R. Swanton, in an article on Louisiana Indian
mythology in *The Journal of American Folk-Lore,*
vol. 20 (1907), summarizes the Chitimacha tale of
"The Great Flood." In vol. 26 (1939), in an article on animal stories, he recounts the tale of
"Rabbit and Wildcat."

*In *Myths and Tales of the Southeastern Indians* (1995),
reprinted from *B.A.E. Bulletin,* no. 88 (1929), Mr.
Swanton includes versions of "Rabbit's Horse,"
"Panther and Little Sister," "Fox and Crawfish,"
"Heron and Hummingbird," "Opossum and
Her Children," "The Wonderful Sky Boat," and
"How Alligator's Nose Was Broken."

Gunter Wagner, in "Yuchi Tales," in *Publications of
the American Ethnological Society,* vol. XIII (1931),
recounts the tale of "The Creation of the World"
in both Yuchi and English.

ABOUT THE AUTHOR

Jane Curry, storyteller and author of over thirty books for young people, was born in Ohio and grew up there and in Pennsylvania. She studied at Indiana University of Pennsylvania, UCLA, Stanford, and the University of London, and taught writing and children's literature at Stanford before turning to writing full time. She now lives in Los Angeles and London.